A NIGHT DIVINE

DAWN KINZER

For those who help the poor and suffering—

And offer hope where there is despair.

*The King will reply, "Truly I tell you,
whatever you did for one of the least of these
brothers and sisters of mine, you did for me."*

~ Matthew 25:40

One

Friday nights were made for putting the week's grind to rest, and Camryn Tate was eager to leave her schedule-driven day behind. The intimate gathering at the nearby wine bar would provide escape from the latest conflict with her mother. Eva Tate was not only the founder of the successful Tate Modeling Agency, she was also Camryn's boss.

With Thanksgiving checked off the calendar less than twenty-four hours ago, "I'll Be Home for Christmas" played softly in the elevator as it descended from the fifty-fourth floor, which housed the agency, to the first, soothing Camryn's nerves. She and her mother had disagreed on a last-minute job offer—a photo shoot in New York on December 24. Why couldn't Mom understand that Camryn didn't want to spend Christmas away from home?

Her mother was welcome to party with colleagues, but Camryn wanted to enjoy the holiday with her dad, sister, and brother-in-law, especially now that her relationship with Liana felt sisterly again after years of friction between them. She'd missed the close friendship they'd shared as little girls, and recognizing her part in their rift, Camryn now welcomed opportunities that helped rebuild what had once been demolished.

The doors slid open, and Camryn stepped into the open-spaced lobby, where three twelve-foot artificial trees stood adorned in white, silver, and crystal ornaments. The clear lights, draped perfectly on the branches, twinkled like a star-studded sky on a cloudless night.

Camryn still appreciated her father's tradition of cutting down a Douglas fir on the family's estate outside of Seattle. The evergreen filled his home with an enticing fresh scent, and he insisted the tree be covered with messy handmade ornaments Camryn and Liana had created over the years. It was no secret that their surgeon father was sentimental beneath his professional exterior.

Ignoring the curious stares, Camryn strolled past several people waiting in line at the lobby's coffee stand. Funny. She used to soak in the attention her camera-ready appearance drew, but now she swallowed hard at the envy in their eyes. She'd learned so much about herself this past year and the shallow life she'd once led. For years Camryn had been self-absorbed, and that revelation had created inner shame and emptiness.

Determined to shift from that unhealthy mindset, she'd spent considerable time contemplating mental, emotional, and yes, even spiritual changes that needed to take place. Her dad was facilitating the God piece, and she'd even started attending church with him several times a month.

George, the building's night security guard, stopped Camryn before she ventured farther. "Ms. Tate, I wanted to warn you. There's . . . *someone* waiting for you outside."

Why would anyone choose standing in the cold over finding a comfortable chair or grabbing a latte at the Starbucks inside?

"She said you're old friends . . ." George could intimidate when required, but at the moment, his compassionate eyes revealed the soft heart beneath his stocky chest. "I tried to convince her to wait inside where it's warm, but I don't think she could face—*this.*"

He nodded toward the row of elevators spewing out professionals with laptop cases slung over their shoulders and cell phones in hand. Overheard conversations relayed last-minute business details and discussions on picking up children from day care and dinner options.

Camryn glanced at her watch.

George tilted his head and eyed her. "You in a hurry? I can show you where to slip out another door if you got plans."

"I do—Eddie Martinez landed a magazine ad for a men's cologne, so there's a little party down the street." Camryn would toast her friend's success and then head home to her comfortable condo on Mercer Island and get some rest.

But if she didn't find out who wanted to talk to her outside and why, it would plague her thoughts all evening. And she was working on putting others first, right?

She smiled at the guard. "Thanks, George, for offering to help me escape, but I can take a minute and see what this person wants. Have a good night." Camryn's heels clicked on the marble floor as she maneuvered around a frazzled-looking woman trying to find her ringing cell phone buried in her purse.

Camryn envied Eddie's enthusiasm for modeling. She used to feel the same way, but lately she hungered for something more. But where would she find it?

Liana stood firm that God had a plan for Camryn's life. If so, it sure would be nice if she'd receive a map with his strategy explained in black and white.

November evenings brought cool temperatures to Seattle, and as Camryn stepped outside, a breeze chilled her bare legs.

Leaves swirled around her ankles, and with her hair twisted up into a side bun, her neck was exposed to the wind blowing in from Puget Sound. The earthy smell in the air hinted a fast-approaching storm. Shivers raced through her body, and she drew her warm wrap around her. Her short sequined dress that sparkled like polished rubies was appropriate for a party, but it didn't protect from the damp cold.

"Camryn?" The hesitant whisper came from a bedraggled figure leaning against the building, which may have offered a hint of shelter from the blustery weather. The slight woman, dressed in tattered jeans, tennis shoes, and a dirty hooded brown jacket pushed away from the structure and shuffled, as if in physical pain, toward Camryn. In one hand she carried a filthy tan canvas bag. The city's festive lights dispelled the shadows on the woman's face.

"Amy? What are you doing here?" Camryn and Amy Farell were only sixteen when Camryn's mother agreed to represent the young woman who showed up with no résumé, no portfolio, and only a few candid shots. It had been at least two years since Camryn had last seen her friend. For her to show up now ...

"I . . . I need help, Cami." Amy wiped her nose with her coat sleeve.

"I can't . . ." It hurt to say those few words, as though she'd had to force them through shards stuck in her throat. Camryn would remain firm. She couldn't cave in. *Not again.* Not even when Amy used the fond nickname she'd given Camryn. "I've tried before. Many times. Remember?"

A text pinged Camryn's cell, and she pulled it from her purse. Eddie wanting to know if she was on her way. She typed a quick response, then slid the phone back in place.

"Your boyfriend?"

"No—a friend." There was a time when Amy would have known about Camryn's broken engagement and that her shattered heart hadn't fully mended. But Amy had lost her place as Camryn's confidante years ago.

The hood slipped from Amy's head, and before she hid beneath it again, Camryn glimpsed her sunken cheeks and pale skin marked with sores. Camryn stifled a gasp. Amy was sick—*really* sick.

"Oh, Amy . . . I'm so sorry," Camryn whispered.

"Did you get my messages?" Amy's voice hitched, as though she could succumb to tears with her next breath. "You never called back."

"I couldn't . . ." Every time Camryn believed Amy wanted to get better, she'd taken advantage of Camryn's generosity. So she'd ended the friendship and cut herself loose from the insanity. As far as she knew, Amy had been living on the streets for the past three years. She'd lost her career—she'd lost everything—because of her addictive behaviors.

Amy's body trembled.

Camryn clutched her wrap tighter and fought the urge to hug the frail woman. Surrounded by bright, cheerful lights strewn along the city streets and store windows filled with colorful holiday designs, everything about Amy's appearance and situation felt out of place.

A Salvation Army Santa Claus rang a bell at the corner of the block, calling out for people to support those in need. Camryn could pass by the familiar red bucket and drop in a few dollars. Or she could take another chance on the person standing right in front of her, begging for support.

But their history—all the times Amy had betrayed Camryn or let her down. Camryn shuddered as the damp air penetrated her body. What was the right thing to do? "How long have you been standing out here in this freezing weather?"

"I don't know. Maybe an hour, maybe two. I lose track of time. I called the agency, but the receptionist wouldn't tell me if you were here. I didn't have anywhere else to go, so I hung around and waited."

"Amy . . ." What should Camryn say? What could she possibly do?

"I want to get better this time. I really do, Cami." Amy fidgeted. "See, there's this guy—Trace."

"You don't need a guy, Amy," Camryn said firmly. How many times had Amy fallen for the wrong man and gotten deeper in trouble? "You need rehab."

"It's not like that. Sometimes he gives me stuff. But he never asks for anything. He just talks to me, and I want to believe what he's saying."

"What do you mean?" Camryn didn't trust that a man would give her friend "stuff" without expecting anything in return. At least, not the type of man Amy had hung out with the last time Camryn had spotted her downtown. Camryn had kept her distance and pretended not to notice her former friend. It was too painful to see Amy in bad shape, knowing there was nothing she could do to help someone who didn't want to change.

Amy shifted her bag from one shoulder to the other. "I know I need to get clean. But rehab—the really good ones—cost a bundle." Amy sniffed. "I don't have that kind of money. I don't have a job. Everything I own is in this bag."

She crossed her arms and held her sides, as though in pain. "C'mon, Cami. You know I don't have anywhere else to go. It's not like I have rich parents like you. If I could borrow what I need . . ." she pleaded in a childish, whiny tone. "You're doing great—you won't even miss it. You can admit me into rehab yourself. Even pick the place. And once I'm better, I'll get a job and pay you back. I promise."

Amy sounded frantic, and maybe she was sincere about finally dealing with her addictions. Past experiences, common sense, and emotions battled, beating up Camryn's insides. Dare she hope and trust that her friend could turn things around—even after living on the streets and making horrible, frightening choices? Could Amy make something of her life again if she tried hard enough?

"*Please*, Cami . . ."

"I can't deal with this right now, Amy. It's too much to ask for me to make a decision when you show up unexpected." Camryn took a deep breath. "I need a little time to think." And her dad would also suggest that she pray—*a lot*. "My cell number is the same. Call tomorrow if you're still serious about rehab, and I'll give you an answer."

"Thank you . . ." Amy grasped Camryn's hand and squeezed, her body shaking again.

Camryn slipped her hand from the woman's desperate grasp and then took several steps in the opposite direction. A soft thud sounded behind Camryn.

Amy had crumpled to the ground.

Two

Camryn dropped next to her friend, her knees on the hard, frigid sidewalk. "Amy!" No response. "Amy!" Camryn put her ear to the other woman's mouth.

"What's going on?" George yelled from the building's entrance. "She all right?"

"She's breathing. But barely."

"I'm calling 911!"

As Camryn cradled Amy's head and shoulders in her lap, the young woman's bones beneath her thin jacket dug into Camryn's arms. Her eyes stung, and her vision blurred. Although her heart pleaded with her to pray, words wouldn't come. Amy had once been naturally beautiful, spunky, and determined to make something of herself. And now . . . Camryn squeezed her eyes shut. A wasted life.

"Can I help?" an earnest, rich male voice asked.

Camryn opened her eyes.

A man with dark hair knelt next to her, and his hazel eyes held hers for only a moment before fixing them on Amy. "What happened?"

"I don't know. We were talking, and then she collapsed." Camryn's hands shook. How much should she relay to this stranger? "A security guard is calling 911."

"Good." He leaned over Amy and checked her breathing and heart. He unwrapped a wool scarf from his neck, doubled it over, and placed it on the ground next to Camryn. "We can't wait for an ambulance. Carefully lay her head there."

What did he mean they couldn't wait? Was Amy in worse shape than Camryn had guessed? She lifted Amy's shoulders and moved her to a prone position, and he immediately began CPR. Camryn remained transfixed on the handsome man who was completely focused on rescuing Amy.

Something luscious and warm fell around her quaking shoulders. George had brought several blankets, and he covered Amy's lower body with one. Where had he found them stashed in the building?

Several small groups of people stood nearby, watching. A siren blared as first responders finally pulled up to the curb. Two people in uniform jumped out the back of the truck. They knelt next to Amy and took over, checking her vital signs and continuing CPR.

Camryn gave the two men what little information she had, and then before she had time to fully absorb what had taken place, they'd loaded Amy onto a stretcher and wheeled her to the back of the truck. George assisted Camryn to her feet, her legs stiff from kneeling on the cold ground. She picked up Amy's bag, which had slid a few feet away when she collapsed, and strode to the rescue vehicle as fast as her heels allowed.

"Where are you taking her?"

"Northwest Medical Center."

One EMT closed the doors, and the vehicle drove off with its lights and siren turned on. What a contrast—the red flashing globes on the truck announcing that someone's life was in danger, and the colorful illuminations that bedecked the city sidewalks and buildings meant to bring cheer.

Camryn still clutched Amy's bag. She should have sent it with the EMTs. Once they'd arrived, everything had moved so fast.

George rubbed his brow. "Quite a night, huh?"

"Yeah," Camryn said with a heavy breath. "Quite a night." She glanced around the well-lit area. "The man who tended Amy—did you see where he went?"

"He took off after the EMTs put your friend in the ambulance."

"Odd that he didn't introduce himself." The man might have saved Amy's life, and Camryn didn't even get a chance to thank him.

She had her car, and the hospital was only a few minutes away. Eddie would understand her decision to miss the party. Camryn almost choked on an unexpected sob. What if Amy didn't survive?

"I explained, miss. *Several* times. I can't give out any information on the patient." The receptionist with purple-rimmed eyeglasses at the desk in the hospital emergency room glared at Camryn.

"And I explained *three* times. She *has* no family. None. Parents are deceased. I'm her only friend in the world, and I was with her when she literally dropped to the ground." Why couldn't the woman understand? Fury stirred up inside like a tornado, and Camryn was tempted to toss the poinsettia sitting on the ledge between them, but she refrained. Throwing a tantrum wouldn't accomplish anything positive. *Keep your cool, Camryn.*

"Look. My father, Dr. Jonathan Tate, is a surgeon at this hospital. That should count for something." Name dropping wasn't new to Camryn, but she never dreamed she'd use her own father's reputation to her advantage. "He'll vouch for me, and he knows the patient. Call him if you need to."

Camryn's father hadn't seen Amy for years, but the irritant behind the desk didn't need to know that. At one time Amy had been like family, and Dad wasn't likely to ever forget her later infamous history when it came to her relationship with Camryn.

"Your father is Dr. Tate?" An older, slightly pudgy gray-haired nurse carrying a stack of files sauntered up behind cranky Purple Frames. Her name tag said *Karen*.

"Yes."

"What's the patient's name?"

"Amy Farell. She was brought in a short time ago." Maybe now Camryn would get some answers.

She pulled Amy's wallet from her canvas bag. "Here's her driver's license. It's long been expired, and I know she no longer lives at that address, but at least it's a photo ID. She doesn't have any money or a job, so there's no health insurance. I'll take financial responsibility." Camryn took a deep breath, and ignoring Purple Frames, peered into the nurse's eyes. "I don't expect details. I'm only asking if she's okay."

Karen nodded. "I'll see what I can find out. But it may take a while, so grab a seat in the waiting area. I'll let you know what's going on as soon as I can."

Camryn sighed with relief. "Thank you. I won't leave until I talk to you."

An empty chair sat between a mother with a crying toddler and a burly man with a bloody bandage wrapped around his arm. The guy, talking nonstop, seemed oblivious that the lady on the other side of him appeared engrossed in her paperback novel. That spot—not a good idea. Better hope for another vacancy.

A guy in hospital garb called a man's name, and Camryn glanced around the room. A middle-aged woman assisted an elderly gentleman to his feet and then held his elbow as he shuffled toward the employee holding a chart. Camryn scooted over and slid into the abandoned seat next to a small Christmas tree decorated with gold garland, crimson balls, and twinkling colored lights. *Merry Christmas . . .*

A teenage boy, sprawled in a chair across from her, stared—his eyes almost popping out. Camryn pulled her hemline down. A woman sitting next to him, probably his mother, gave her an odd look. Dressed in sequins, Camryn did look out of place in the ER. She draped her wrap over her shoulders and covered as much of her body as possible, regretting not wearing the knee-length dress originally chosen.

The clock on the wall displayed the current time as 8:27 p.m., but it felt like 2:27 a.m. Now that Camryn could do nothing but wait, exhaustion flooded her body. Her shoulder muscles ached, as did her head. Because she'd planned to indulge at the restaurant that evening, she'd only eaten oatmeal with raisins for breakfast and a small apple for lunch. She should be ravenous, but her appetite had waned. Camryn's nerves were near the edge.

God, if you're listening, please, please watch over Amy. She has to be okay. She just has to ...

Guilt influenced Camryn to pray. Amy had begged for help. But Camryn had justified turning her friend away at that moment—enough was enough. Instead of Amy following through on any previous agreements, she'd failed repeatedly.

Second chances were important, and Camryn had given

Amy three, four, and many more. Pastors and therapists pretty much all said the same thing during interviews on TV talk shows. Actions necessitated consequences.

Karen, the nurse who'd offered to check on Amy, stood off to the side of the room, holding two steaming cups, searching. She caught Camryn's eye and hiked over.

"I needed caffeine and took a chance you might too." Karen handed her a cup, then slid into the empty chair next to Camryn's.

"Thanks." Holding hot coffee in her hands felt comforting. "Any word?"

The nurse shook her head. "No, I'm sorry. I don't have anything to report. It's a busy night, as usual. But I wanted you to know I hadn't forgotten you." She laid her free hand on Camryn's shoulder. "And I also wanted you to know that I'm praying for your friend."

"You think praying makes a difference?" Camryn wanted all the reassurance she could get.

Karen smiled. "I *know* it does." She patted Camryn's arm. "I need to get back to work. I was lucky to get five minutes to visit the restroom."

"Thanks." Camryn managed a feeble smile.

The nurse smiled in return, then left.

The teenage boy continued to gawk. He didn't appear sick. If only he'd leave and free her from his uncomfortable stare.

Camryn set her coffee cup down and grabbed a handful of magazines from the low-standing table in front of her and sifted through them. Her stomach flipped. Her photo—on July's torn front cover of *Elle*. At the time, that shot had made her proud. The dress's aquamarine color matched her eyes, the stylist said her blond hair looked like sunshine, and the spray tan made her skin glow. Those descriptions didn't quite fit the mustache and goatee now drawn on her face with magic marker. Red-penned dots gave her either a bad case of acne or the measles. *Nice.*

She shoved the magazine under the pile. What a legacy.

God, what am I supposed to do? I'm not the smartest person on the planet. But I'm intelligent enough to know that I need more than an airbrushed photo to give my life meaning.

Maybe God had already answered. Maybe he'd wanted Camryn to be there for Amy all along. Maybe this time things would work out and Amy would shake her addictions and become her old self again. She'd need to get healthy, but with Camryn's support, Amy could even model again. Not for the larger magazines. She'd damaged working relationships beyond repair in that arena, but there might be catalog work. Hard work and determination—that was all she'd need.

And *hope.*

Camryn's sister, brother-in-law, and father all attended the same church. After seeing how relaxed and at peace Liana had been since embracing a deeper faith, Camryn had decided it was time to rethink her own limited beliefs. Maybe by showing up only on Easter and Christmas, she was missing out on something valuable. Her dad had been trying to convince her of that for some time, and she'd finally agreed.

One of the times she'd attended church services the past several months, the topic had been hope and how it could make a difference. That was exactly what Amy needed—*hope.*

Hearing a commotion, Camryn's gaze returned to the receptionist's desk. Who was Purple Frames harassing now? The gentleman leaned across the top of the desk. Was he going to strangle the woman with his scarf? *Wait*—that red wool scarf. Was he here to check on Amy? Or was another patient admitted because of his heroics?

Camryn headed in his direction—partly because she felt it her duty to spare him Purple Frames's condescension, but mostly because she wanted to thank him for coming to Amy's rescue. She reached the desk as he turned to leave. "Hello."

He glanced back, then faced her. "Hi." Those gorgeous eyes with flecks of green and gold squinted as though he was trying to place her. *Really?* Only a few hours earlier, they'd knelt beside each other while working to keep someone alive. Recognition filled his face. "Oh, sorry. You were with the woman who collapsed on the sidewalk."

She held out her hand. "Camryn Tate."

"Trace," he said as they shared a quick shake. His smile lit up Camryn's insides like a Christmas display at Enchant Seattle.

"I'm glad I got a chance to thank you." Unexpected emotion swelled from within, and Camryn could barely choke out the words.

"No need to say thanks." That smile again. He nodded toward Purple Frames. "I knew there wasn't much chance she'd give me even a hint of how your friend was doing, but I had to try."

"I ran into the same thing because of HIPAA compliance. But I have friends in high places here, so I'm still hoping to get word soon." However long it took, Camryn would stay until assured Amy would recover.

"I need to head out and finish an earlier commitment, but I'm glad I ran into you." Trace reached into his back pocket for his wallet. He removed a business card and handed it to her. "I'd appreciate a call—let me know if she's okay."

"Sure," Camryn said, dropping the card into her small purse without reading it.

"Thanks. I'll be praying for her." Trace gave a quick wave, then walked out the door.

She returned to her chair in the waiting area. *Praying? Was Trace a man or a Christmas angel in disguise?*

"Ms. Tate?"

Camryn snapped out of her thoughts. "Yes?" One look into Karen's sad eyes, and Camryn's throat closed. The kind nurse's face blurred before her.

"I'm sorry. They tried everything . . . Her body was too worn out, and her organs shut down." Karen put an arm around Camryn's shoulder. "Are you sure there isn't family somewhere?"

"There's no one. Her grandparents passed a long time ago. Her mother died when Amy was nineteen. No siblings. She never knew her father . . ."

"And you? Anyone you'd like me to call?"

Camryn closed her eyes and shook her head. "No. Thank you. You've been kind and generous with your time." A tissue was placed in her hand, and she wiped her nose, now threatening to drip. She blinked her eyes and peered up at the nurse who had been understanding. "May I see her?"

"Let me check." The nurse squeezed Camryn's shoulder and left on her mission.

This wasn't supposed to happen. This wasn't how Amy's life was supposed to end. Maybe if Camryn had done more or attempted something different. *Why didn't I try harder?*

She wiped her eyes and blew her nose with the damp tissue. Camryn's foot bumped against the canvas bag propped against the chair, so she picked it up and held it against her chest. The boy sitting across the room still watched her, but this time he wasn't ogling her as much as he looked concerned.

The tote didn't contain much, but each item now carried significance for Camryn. They were Amy's only belongings. Camryn fingered a tattered copy of *To Kill a Mockingbird*. A plastic bag containing a toothbrush and a small tube of toothpaste. A comb. A brush. Her wallet that held two one-dollar bills and eighty-five cents in change. A few pieces of jewelry, including her mother's locket, were tucked inside a carved wooden box.

Photos were stored in a second plastic bag. Camryn sifted through them. Shots included Amy and her mother sharing a picnic, Amy's sixth birthday, copies of her first cover shoot, and Camryn and Amy together in Hawaii after they'd both turned twenty-one. Camryn swiped moisture from her cheek. She should have waited for the privacy of her condo before searching her friend's things.

Camryn's fingers grasped a thin object at the bottom of the bag. A business card for Trace Gardner—Community Outreach. The information included the name of a church, the address, and a phone number.

Trace was the name of the man Amy had mentioned. Wasn't it also the name of the guy who had shown up on the sidewalk when she struggled to hold on to life? Coincidence? Camryn compared the business card he'd given her only minutes earlier and the one in Amy's bag. *Identical.*

Moisture filled Camryn's eyes. What was she supposed to think? Feel? How could the man whom Amy had trusted be the same Trace Gardner who had come to her aid tonight?

Why would he act like he'd never met Amy before? None of it made any sense.

Three

The aroma of coffee brewing filled his office. The new single-cup makers were fast and convenient, but Trace appreciated the pot he'd picked up for a few bucks that still did the job. He'd rather pour spare cash into the street ministry than spend it on a high-end coffee gadget.

Trace rubbed his tired eyes. If more donations didn't come in soon for their meal program, he'd have to hit up local stores. Trace would also visit congregations in the Seattle area and other organizations that funded charities. Standing in front of a crowd—even a small group—and asking for money wasn't his *thing*. But in his determination to meet people's needs, he'd do almost anything to raise money. Well, anything that was legal and wouldn't harm anyone.

No matter how many times he went over the spreadsheet and added up the numbers, he didn't have enough to keep his programs running. Most people who attended Abundant Life Church and lived in the inner-city community survived on minimum-wage jobs, small savings, and social security. They'd already given much. How could he ask more of them?

Without a doubt they'd give an abundance—if they had it to give. The congregation believed in what he was hoping to accomplish with renovating the old building across the street from the church into a shelter with an educational wing and day care facility. With that resource in place, they could facilitate transition off the streets. Train the homeless for specific jobs and assist them with finding housing. Trace had a vision, but ongoing obstacles had halted that dream coming to fruition.

The Union Gospel Mission, a well-respected ministry, provided various supplies and resources for those living on the Seattle streets, under bridges, and in tent camps. But they couldn't do it all—they couldn't take care of the entire homeless population in the city, now over twelve thousand.

Holiday music blasted from the church secretary's office down the hall. The cheerful tunes didn't cause his headache. They didn't alleviate it either, but he couldn't ask Miss Christmas to turn the sound down. He'd rather endure a little pain than squash any of her enthusiasm.

Melissa Cruz was the most generous person he'd ever met. Not that she donated huge sums to the church or the poor. How could she on her meager salary? But even though she was in her early twenties and had interests outside the church, she still contributed anything she could spare to those in need. And those homemade Christmas cookies shared with all who walked through the doors had to be created from heavenly ingredients and love, because they melted in your mouth.

His email had gone unchecked for several hours. Maybe Trace would discover a rich benefactor had decided to bequeath part of his fortune. A weak chuckle slipped through his lips. He could hope, couldn't he? Out of habit, Trace picked up his cell to check for notifications. A voice message. Why hadn't he heard the call?

Two words into the playback, he released a long sigh. His father had probably gotten Trace's unlisted phone number from the church secretary. Trace couldn't blame her—he'd given the woman permission to give out his cell number to anyone who asked. He wanted to be accessible to the people he was trying to serve.

Trace tapped the phone several times to his forehead. At some point, they'd need to talk again, but Trace wasn't ready to call his father. Too much had happened—too much had been lost. How was he supposed to find resolution when his dad wouldn't accept Trace's decision to leave the family business?

"Excuse me." Camryn—that was her name—stood in his office doorway dressed in tight jeans and a light-pink coat. "You have a few minutes? I know you said to call with news about Amy, but I wanted to tell you in person."

"Sure. Come on in." He stood from behind his desk to greet her. "I'm glad you came."

Camryn's clean, fresh face wasn't plastered with makeup like some of the women he'd encountered on the streets of Seattle late at night. In his past life, wearing expensive clothes was not only the norm but an expectation, so he didn't miss the fact that although she dressed simply, her attire was high end.

Had she been in a jolly holiday state of mind, he imagined her large aquamarine eyes would have sparkled like the sun's reflection on the sea. But those eyes were filled with sadness, and her lips were held in a straight line instead of curved up in laughter.

He shot her a smile and pulled a soft chair closer to his desk. "Can I get you anything to drink? I've got hot coffee and cold water."

"No, nothing. Thank you." She settled in, then chewed her bottom lip, as though trying to decide how to proceed.

"You know, I never got your last name," he said, returning

to his own chair.

"Tate—my last name is Tate."

"Camryn Tate. It's now lodged in my memory." Obviously distraught, she fidgeted in the chair. How could he make her feel more comfortable? Should he encourage her to talk or wait patiently for her to speak? "Camryn, is Amy going to be okay?"

Camryn's eyes brimmed with tears, and she turned away for a moment. Then she took a deep breath, faced him, and handed him a business card.

Trace glanced at the card—*his* card. "I don't understand."

"That's not the card you gave me last night. I found this one in Amy's bag, along with her remaining possessions."

"You did?" He'd never met Amy before—he was sure of it. He frequently forgot names but never faces. Trace studied the card. He could stare at the words for hours and still not make sense out of what his visitor had relayed.

"I'm confused." Camryn cleared her throat. "When Amy approached me last night, she told me about a man named Trace who often talked to her and *gave* her things. I thought it strange that you and her benefactor shared the same name, until I came across the card identical to the one you'd given me."

"I don't know how your friend acquired my information, but I promise it didn't come from me." Trace tapped the card on his desk, thinking. "There's one possibility ..."

That had to be the explanation. Trace couldn't think of another scenario. "I'm a volunteer with the Union Gospel Mission. Search and Rescue vans go out at night and park in various areas in the city. UGM has built a reputation on the streets, so the homeless find the vans, and we hand out food, water, blankets, and other supplies. Then we offer shelter—one location for men and another for women."

"What has that got to do with Amy?"

"Sometimes people aren't ready to accept help—or they may want assistance but are not willing to obey the shelter's rules. The homeless population has grown in Seattle, and one organization can't support everyone. So part of my role here at the church is developing additional programs. We hand out food on the streets, and we also provide meals here in the evening several times a week.

"A couple of months ago, one of my friends—another volunteer—asked if he could pass out a few of my cards. I gave him a handful, but we haven't talked about it since. Jerry is a good guy. If he gave Amy my card, he thought there was a chance she'd call or come by—maybe drop in for one of our free meals. She must have assumed his name was Trace."

"I guess that makes sense." Camryn relaxed into the chair. "I'm sorry . . ."

"You have nothing to apologize for."

"I judged too quickly in thinking you'd kept a connection to Amy a secret. I even worried there might have been unsavory ties between you two."

"And now?" Did Camryn still mistrust him? He would never have done anything to hurt Amy. His life was devoted to caring for those who didn't know how to love themselves.

"I'm relieved that I came to find out for myself." Her lips parted, as though she had more to relay, but Camryn bowed her head in silence. Praying? Or working up the courage to say what else was on her mind?

Camryn lifted her gaze, and those beautiful eyes filled with pain. "Amy died last night."

"Oh, Camryn, I'm sorry . . ." His heart clenched, as though reacting to a strong punch. Another soul had lost the battle with addiction and the chance to create a new and better life for herself—one that was healthy and whole. Trace had witnessed far too many tragedies on the streets, so he wasn't surprised to learn of Amy's death, but he'd still prayed that she might be spared. He mourned within because he knew the loss also grieved their heavenly Father.

"I hadn't seen Amy in a long time, but when she found me last night, she tried to convince me she was ready to get clean." Camryn's chin trembled, and several tears escaped. She wiped the moisture from her cheeks. "I wanted to believe her."

"She might have been trying, but addiction can maintain a strong hold." He wasn't proud of it, but Trace knew intimately the destructive grip drugs and alcohol could have on a person.

"Amy lied, stole from me, and betrayed me numerous times. I gave her many chances to redeem herself, but I'm not a professional." Camryn shook her head in a way that exhibited her feeling of defeat. "I didn't know how to save her."

"You're not to blame for Amy's struggles, and it's not your fault she died." Trace leaned forward on his desk. "It's still hard for me to accept that I can't fix anyone. I can only offer assistance if the person wants to work at getting healed."

"I appreciate your kindness." Camryn sounded sincere and slightly broken. "Even though you asked for a call and update, I had no right to come here and burden you with this." She sighed as her eyes pooled again. "Amy has no family, so I'm making any necessary arrangements."

"You and Amy were close." It was a statement, but it hinted the door was open if Camryn wanted to share more. Trace could only imagine all the thoughts and feelings that coursed through her.

"Once. A long time ago—before getting high was more important than friendship, work, or anything else." Camryn eyed the coffeepot on the nearby counter. "Could I take you up on your offer now?"

"Sure." Trace poured a steaming cup and handed it to her. "It's not Starbucks with all the works, but it's strong and hot."

"Thanks." She embraced the mug as though it were nourishment from heaven.

He filled another for himself, then dropped into his own chair. She seemed deep in thought, so he remained silent and glanced at his watch. Only five minutes before he was due in an important church staff meeting, but he couldn't push Camryn out the door—not when she was grieving. Pastor and the rest would offer him grace.

"Tell me more."

"Amy and I met when we were teenagers." Camryn peered at him over her raised cup. "We worked together and became good friends—almost like sisters. But after she started using drugs, it grew more difficult for her to even show up at a job." Camryn cleared her throat. "I convinced her to enter rehab, but if she wanted to get better, she didn't want it enough.

"The stealing and constant lying became intolerable. No one trusted her at that point. Her mom had passed by then." She took another sip of coffee. "I've heard of the Union Gospel Mission, but I guess I never paid too much attention to what people did there. And then to learn that you're also providing aid through your own work . . ."

Camryn studied him with admiration shining in her eyes. "I'm glad I was wrong about you, Trace Gardner."

It boosted his ego but made him uncomfortable at the same time. If she knew his personal story, she might not be so trusting of his character.

❧

"What can I do to help?" Excitement filled Camryn's voice. Maybe it was guilt over not providing more for Amy when she had the chance. Maybe she was caught up in the holiday spirit. Or maybe listening to Trace talk about the homeless ministry inspired her. Regardless, she wanted to dig in.

Trace leaned back in his chair, regarding her with questioning hazel eyes. "Are you sure you know what you're asking?"

He might be good looking—okay, ruggedly handsome with his tousled dark-brown hair and broad shoulders—but he wasn't going to intimidate her or dismiss her.

"Look. I understand that you don't know me . . ."

"You're right. I don't know a thing about you except that you're loyal to your friends. That goes a long way with me. If you're interested in finding a way to be charitable during the holidays, I know a lot of people who would be grateful, including myself. You might be surprised at what even a small donation can accomplish."

Camryn's face heated. "Pardon?" Did he think she merely wanted to write out a check? Had she been wrong about him?

"I didn't mean that I expected you to give money—I don't know what I expected."

"So when you made that comment, you had no idea that my family has a large bank account?"

"What? No." Trace scooted forward in his chair. "Absolutely

not."

He sounded sincere. When would Camryn stop assuming that people were more interested in her family's money than her? "Trust me. I wasn't talking about making a financial contribution. I'm not asking to help because I think it will make me feel better about Amy. I'm not trying to be some do-gooder, and I have no aspirations of becoming Santa Claus."

"Okay. You have my attention. I believe you."

Could she be completely honest with him? Could she let down her guard and not worry about being judged?

"I don't know what I have to offer that will encourage people or make their lives better. But I'm willing to try—I *need* to try." Camryn couldn't go on feeling empty inside—with no purpose other than representing companies who sold promises to women. Perhaps this would be a good place to begin. "When can I start volunteering with your program?"

Trace raised his eyebrows, then he gave her a satisfied smile. "A small group of us hands out lunches downtown on Mondays, Wednesday, and Fridays. We meet here around ten to make sandwiches and pack bags."

"I have a meeting first thing that morning, so I won't make it by then." Camryn checked the calendar on her phone. "What time do you leave here?"

"We're usually ready to head out by eleven thirty."

"Count me in."

Four

T race took a moment to observe the volunteer team, and his heart filled with gratitude. This crew liked working together, which was a blessing, since they'd remained his Monday regulars. They kept conversation flowing as they checked in with each other and shared updates about their lives. This was ministry at its best—when those who served were fed not only with food but also friendship.

A few more lunch bags to pack with sandwiches, apples, and cookies, and they'd be on their way. The additional toiletry items recently added to the donation bin would also be welcomed. They never seemed to have enough soap, toothpaste, and toothbrushes to fill the need.

"Trace, someone is here to see you." With a big grin on her face, Melissa Cruz, the church secretary, stood next to Camryn.

"Hi." Did he sound as shocked as he felt? Trace hadn't expected Camryn to show up. Sure, when she'd dropped in to see him last Saturday, she'd offered to lend a hand, but people changed their minds all the time after committing to projects that weren't going to benefit them in some tangible way.

The team glanced in Camryn's direction, then continued filling cardboard boxes with lunches and supplies.

"I'm sorry I didn't get here earlier, but I explained about the meeting." Camryn's forehead furrowed as she dropped a large canvas bag on the floor. "You didn't think I'd forgotten, did you?"

"No. Of course not." Trace opened his mouth, then shut it. Better to stop while ahead. But how was she going to manage walking the cold streets in those clothes? She looked amazing, but the formfitting dress, heels, and red leather jacket weren't appropriate for their mission.

"Give me a minute to change." Camryn picked up the bag and swung it over her shoulder. "Don't leave me behind."

Relief that she'd come prepared washed over him like a cool breeze on a sweltering day. He had to stop assuming things about Camryn—she kept proving him wrong. "We still need to finish up here. Go ahead, and when you get back, I'll introduce you to the rest of the team." Trace smiled and nodded toward the crew.

"The ladies' room is down there and to the right," Melissa said, pointing. "I can show you, if you'd like."

"Oh, thanks, but I can find it." Camryn shifted her bag and headed down the hall.

Melissa grinned. "Trace, you didn't tell me you'd talked a celebrity into volunteering."

He picked up an empty cardboard box and placed it on the table for personal items they'd distribute. "I have no idea what you're talking about."

"Seriously? Camryn Tate?" Melissa sighed. "I need to get some things from the office." In less than a minute, the secretary returned with several magazines. She held two covers in front of his face. "*This!* Your new volunteer is one of the top models in the country, and her entire family is well known."

And there she was—in one photo, dressed in a gown with a long skirt made from feathers and a top covered with se-quins. In the other, she wore a red sweater and black slacks while posing with an ornament in front of a Christmas tree. Camryn must have thought him completely out of touch to have not recognized her. How could he have known? It wasn't like he read fashion magazines or even paid attention to any type of publication while waiting in line at the grocery store.

He turned around, and there she stood—now wearing jeans, a cream-colored sweater, and boots. She'd removed the bright-red lipstick, and her face looked freshly washed. Instead of the leather jacket, Camryn carried a thicker black coat. Her gaze moved to the magazines in Melissa's hands.

The secretary held up the publications. "I recognized you the minute you walked in. I love your photos."

"Thank you. That's very kind of you." Camryn gave a weak smile. "But credit goes to the photographer."

"Well, anyway, these covers are gorgeous, and so are you." Melissa shot another exuberant grin at Trace, then picked up on his *let's move on* signal. "I better get back to work. Pastor doesn't like phone calls to go unanswered." She turned back to Camryn. "It's nice having you here." Then she headed toward the office.

Trace caught Camryn's eye. "Why didn't you tell me?"

"The other day when you mentioned donations, you honestly didn't know anything about my family?"

"I had no idea. And now I'm rather embarrassed by what I said—and being naïve about your work."

"It's actually refreshing that you weren't aware." Camryn sighed. "I'd appreciate it if you and the rest of the team didn't make a big deal out of my profession—or my family connections. I'd like to be treated like any other volunteer."

"Sure." Trace had become intrigued about this woman who graced magazine covers yet seemed humble. There must be more to her family's story too. "Let me introduce you to everyone before we head out." He walked over to the end of the table and waved at the people assembling kits. "Hey, team, I want you to meet Camryn. She'll be joining us today."

Had she made the right decision? It seemed like a good idea a few days ago, but now standing in front of a small group, ready to venture out on the streets of Seattle and talk to strangers, Camryn's stomach felt like angry bees swarmed within.

"Hi, everyone," Camryn said, her voice slightly squeaking. Why was she nervous? She'd traveled and met people from all over the world without faltering. But in her role, she'd presented a certain persona. Today, she was only Camryn, and that was how she wanted it. She received warm smiles and welcoming greetings from the group.

"Camryn, meet Martha Strand, the woman with a heart of gold and the best hugger in the Seattle area." Trace put his arm around a silver-haired woman with blue eyes. She wore a Christmas sweater with a tree knitted in the design. Martha reminded Camryn of the fairy godmother in Cinderella—a little plump, but cheerful and spry.

The lean man with salt-and-pepper hair was introduced as Michael Laud. Trace mentioned that Michael was a retired math teacher who still ran three miles a day.

"Hi, I'm Sherrie Kern." The woman with curly red hair, brown eyes, and freckles grinned at Camryn.

"Are you three regular volunteers?" If Camryn decided to come back, there might be some comfort in working with the same team.

Martha nodded. "Sherrie, Michael, and I try to be here every Monday. Occasionally, we cover other days too."

"I come as often as I can." Sherrie picked up the remaining filled bags and packed them in a box. "My two kids are in college, and I work part time as an accountant from a home office, so my schedule is somewhat flexible."

The team was a mix of personalities, but they all seemed nice. Camryn's stomach settled down, and her aching shoulders relaxed.

"I'm glad I caught you before you left." A husky man of about forty-five with dark hair and a trimmed beard strolled in. By his build, he could have been a linebacker for the Seahawks at one time. "We can't send you out without asking the Lord's blessing."

Trace chuckled. "You're just in time. I was about to pray myself, but since you're here . . ." Trace gave the man a gentle slap on the back. "Camryn, meet Pastor Brotherton."

"Nice to meet you." Camryn's hand was enveloped by the pastor's gentle grasp.

"Call me Pastor or TJ," he said with a grin. "Now, let's get to praying so you can get out of here." The pastor reached for Martha's and Camryn's hands.

As Camryn bowed her head, Trace grabbed her free hand and held it firmly during the prayer. With his touch, the bees in her stomach morphed into butterflies.

What was she getting herself into?

Five

C amryn assumed they'd be carrying supplies up and down the streets, but Trace explained that now they'd established a routine, those in need knew where and when to find them. Word spread fast, and new people came in search of food every week.

They parked the van in a lot, then set up a table on the sidewalk where they'd been given permission to serve the homeless community. The team placed lunch bags and hot coffee on one end of the table and kits with personal items on the other end. They stashed bags with sweatshirts, socks, gloves, jackets, and blankets below the covered table. They'd dole those items out at their discretion, along with flyers that gave the church's address and the schedule for meals served there. People lined up, eager to receive, before the team had finished preparations.

Bright sunshine had welcomed the day, but now dark clouds rolled in, a cold breeze picked up, and the threat of rain filled the air. They might get a dusting of snow the following week, but for now the temps were warm enough to ward off any flakes at sea level.

Michael and Sherrie worked together, handing out information and welcoming people as they approached the tables.

"Camryn, would you like to pour coffee?" Trace set out additional stacks of paper cups. "Remind everyone they should take only one lunch bag and one kit with personal items."

"Sure, I can do that." Camryn breathed a sigh of relief. She wouldn't have to approach strangers. But coffee? She could handle that.

"Great. Martha will move between jobs as necessary. I'll pass out clothes, but I also like to give personal attention to as many people as I can. That's an important part of what Michael and Sherrie are doing. They're listening to stories. People need to talk, and they need to be heard. For some it's as critical to their well-being as food and clothing."

This was all a bit foreign to her, but she wasn't going to wimp out, despite her body shivering. In a few hours, *she* could go home to a comfortable, warm home with a refrigerator stocked with healthy vegetables and fruits. How could she complain about temporarily cold toes? She greeted each person who came by the table with a smile, even those who made her feel uncomfortable with their stares and mumblings.

Martha, on the other hand, seemed at ease, and she spoke to each visitor with compassion and respect. Camryn took mental notes. Some must have been regulars, because Martha called them by name and asked personal questions.

The line dwindled, except for a few stragglers. Almost everything had been given away. Trace and Martha were in a deep discussion with a much-wrinkled, hunched-over woman. She pushed a cart that held her possessions—a bag lady they addressed as Mrs. Whitmore.

Camryn rubbed her gloved hands together to keep warm. What was she supposed to do now? It felt odd to stand there idly behind the table while the rest of the team engaged in conversations with street people.

A man dressed in a dirty old coat struggled up the sidewalk

on crutches, appearing exhausted by the effort. Camryn's heart ached for him.

She poured a cup of coffee, grabbed one of the few remaining lunch bags, and met him as he hobbled in her direction. "Sir, would you like to sit down? There's a place over here."

Camryn pointed to the wooden barrier built around the front of the parking lot and the ledge that extended from where the chain link fence was anchored. It wasn't much to sit on, but it was better than the cold ground.

His gaze met hers, and she was taken aback by the clear green eyes and how they lit up at her suggestion. "Thank you. I hurt my ankle the other day, and it's been a little hard getting around since." He chuckled. "I've been using these borrowed crutches to walk longer distances, and to tell you the truth, they're sometimes more of a hindrance."

"I'm sorry to hear that."

"Ahhh . . . for the most part, I'm feeling pretty good, and I'll be back to running marathons in no time. But thank you for your sympathy."

Camryn immediately liked this upbeat gentleman. "Marathons, huh?"

"A man can dream, can't he? What's a world without 'em?" He winked. "Anyway, I heard about what you good people are doing from some of my friends living in the camp under the bridge over there, but I didn't realize how long it would take me to get here with this bum foot."

"Please. Rest. We have food and coffee."

"Something hot to drink would be much appreciated, as well as anything you can spare to eat." The man moved slowly, but he settled in with a heavy sigh and leaned his crutches against the fence.

"Are you sure you're going to be okay? Has a doctor examined you?"

"Can't afford one, but I'll be good as new before you know it," he said, then grinned. "I know I complained about the crutches, but in reality, they've been a godsend."

He opened the lunch bag she handed him and took out the turkey sandwich. *White bread.* Camryn cringed. It was better than nothing but lacked much-essential nutrition. Regardless, the injured man with kind eyes seemed to enjoy the simple meal.

A large hole had worn through his right shoe near the toe, his baggy pants hung loosely on his body, and he could have used a haircut and shave. But there was something about him that drew Camryn in—she just couldn't place it. Trace had said it was important to listen to people's stories. Could she ask questions without appearing intrusive? Maybe start out with something simple.

"I'm Camryn," she said. "I'd shake your hand, but both are full at the moment."

His eyes crinkled in the corners when he smiled. "Nice to meet you, Camryn. I'm Bruce."

"Well, Bruce, I'm glad you found your way here."

"You do this kind of thing often?" He nodded toward the table and the rest of the team who were either still invested in various exchanges or packing up.

"No. First time." A wind gust came through, and a few raindrops fell. Camryn pulled up her hood. "But as you might have heard, a group shows up here every Monday—at least as many as possible. I think they set up at various locations, depending on the day, and the church serves hot meals in the evenings. I could grab you a flyer with the address if you like."

"That's nice of you to offer, but I doubt I'll be going too far for now."

Camryn sat quiet for a moment. "If you don't mind me asking, what's your story, Bruce?"

His forehead furrowed. "You really want to know?"

"I do. And I'll listen for as long as you want to talk." Camryn felt confident the team would wait for her.

Bruce, a fifty-five-year-old veteran, never went to college. After serving in the military, he found work as a factory foreman, but when production slowed down, he was laid off.

"My wife became ill and depended on me to take care of her. She passed away two years ago, but we didn't have health insurance. Paying the bills wiped me out. I tried, but I couldn't get a job. Companies wanted to hire younger guys. You hit your fifties, and suddenly you're incompetent? What's wrong with this world?" he asked, with the first hint of bitterness in his tone.

"I agree. It doesn't seem fair." As a model, Camryn would also face age discrimination with time. One of the reasons she was reassessing her own life. "How long have you been living on the streets?"

"About a year, trying to find work. In and out of shelters. But I've never been a user or a drinker. My wife was religious, and she didn't believe in it. To honor her, I stopped drinking after I married her."

"You're a religious man, Bruce?"

"Nah." He wiped crumbs from his lips. "But I sure prayed a lot while Evie was sick. Even with her dying breath she asked me to accept Jesus into my life. There must be something to it since it was important to her. I just haven't gotten around to it yet."

Bruce scratched his stubble-covered jaw. "Guess I'm still angry and blaming God for what happened to my Evie and my life. I have no idea of what the future will hold, but I've got to believe there's something better than this. Maybe God will fill me in when I get right with him."

And maybe God would get around to letting Camryn know what he wanted for her future as well.

Six

"Hey, Camryn, welcome back." Trace couldn't hide his enthusiasm at seeing her walk through the kitchen door at the church only two days after her initiation to their street ministry. This time she was dressed for the job and had arrived early enough to make lunches.

Her eyes narrowed, and her head tilted slightly, but in a way that made her appear amused. "You sound surprised."

"Sorry—please don't take offense. I assumed you'd be tied up with business." What did models do? Besides stand in front of a camera? Did they work every day? Trace didn't have a clue.

"No offense taken." Her smile lit her face as she slipped off her coat. "Modeling isn't like a nine-to-five job. Some days and weeks are extremely busy, and every hour is filled from early morning until late at night. But I also have days or weeks where I don't have any commitments, and my time is my own."

"Sounds like a nice life."

"It can be, but it's more difficult than what most people believe." Camryn tucked a strand of hair behind her ear, and she seemed to hesitate and think about what to say next. "A lot of girls—women—in the business work several jobs aside from modeling, to make ends meet. I'm one of the lucky ones. I've done well enough in my career, I don't need to juggle occupations."

From the magazine covers the church secretary had shown him, Trace could understand why she'd been successful. Yet she seemed humble. It was . . . unexpected.

Camryn greeted Michael and Sherrie, then clapped her hands together. "Tell me what to do. Where do I start?"

"We're here! We're here. Sorry we're late." Martha bustled in with her sixteen-year-old granddaughter, who had straight dark hair and the same blue eyes as Martha. The girl wore a red Santa hat with a large white puffy ball at the end and a grin as big and bright as a quarter moon.

"Kylie, you have the day off from school?" Trace was pleased to see the girl, who always added enthusiasm to their adventures.

"I sure do. And Gram said I could come along."

"You're always welcome." Trace pulled several more packages of sliced turkey from the fridge. "Michael, if you can grab a box over there on the counter, I'll take the other one. The rest of the supplies are laid out on the tables in the fellowship hall. Kate and Pastor are jumping in for twenty minutes, and they should be here soon. We'll get an assembly line going and have everything made and packed in no time."

Where were his manners? He wanted Camryn to feel welcome, especially when she'd come twice in one week. The ministry depended on volunteers, and he didn't want anyone to feel left out or taken for granted. Michael and Sherrie had greeted Camryn but didn't say much more. Trace should have introduced her to Kylie. Good thing Martha and her granddaughter were extroverts. They were already chatting it up with the newcomer.

He'd only recently met the beautiful woman, but he was already intrigued by Camryn. What was it she'd said about family connections the other day? Was he supposed to know something about her family? He hated gossips and snoops, but maybe this one time, it might be important to learn more about Camryn Tate before he let his attraction grow even stronger. After Nikki broke his heart, he'd made a promise to himself to never get involved with another woman accustomed to a wealthy lifestyle.

&

Camryn's heart skipped a beat. Trace could have found a spot anywhere in the lunch production line, but he stood next to her. He grabbed a loaf of white bread from the box below the table and after removing several pieces, laid them out for her to top with mustard or mayo, then sandwich meat.

"Umm . . ." Camryn tried not to cringe, but she failed.

Trace raised his eyebrows. "Anything wrong? They look fine to me. No mold."

"Really? No mold is what you're going after?" Camryn should weigh her words carefully. She was new at this and didn't want to insult him—he was the leader, after all.

"I'm not sure what *you're* after."

"White bread. There's nothing nutritious about it."

"Oh. I get it. You're one of *those*."

Camryn opened her mouth to spew out a quick comeback, then saw the twinkle in his eyes, and swallowed her retort. Two could play this game, and he wasn't going to get a rise out of her. "Are the homeless not worthy of healthy meals?"

"They not only deserve good nutrition, they need it. But something is better than nothing. We can't afford expensive organic foods. Our program relies on donations, and we do the best we can."

Of course Trace wouldn't give anyone less than what he could provide. "Would it be okay if I checked into a few bakeries that make amazing, hearty whole-grain breads? See if they'd donate day-old products?" She could almost guarantee that several would participate on a regular basis.

"Sure. That would be great. We receive donations from several stores and bakeries now, but they've never been able to provide the healthier options."

A spark lit in Camryn. Maybe there were other creative ways she could contribute.

"Hey, Trace!" Kylie yelled from across the room. "Mind if I put on some music?"

"Sounds good to me. Go ahead."

"Thanks!" Kylie took an MP3 player from her backpack, and soon "Jingle Bell Rock" livened the atmosphere.

Trace opened another bag of bread. "You must have enjoyed Monday's experience to show up again today."

"I did." Bruce had been on her mind since then. Could she—*should* she bring him up now? "The man on crutches the other day . . ."

"Looked like you were comfortable spending time with him."

"His name is Bruce. A nice guy who suffered a few bad breaks." Camryn chuckled at Trace's grin in response to her comment. "And I don't mean that in reference to the crutches."

"So you took my advice and listened to his story."

"I did. He's a vet, and he had a good job, but then he got laid off. His wife got sick, but they didn't have medical insurance at the time. With all the bills adding up . . ."

Trace sighed. "He lost everything."

"He's fighting his way back, and he wants to work, but at his age . . . Anyway, he's living in one of the tent camps." She was new to this, and maybe she didn't have a right to ask, but something nudged her to go ahead. "Do you think there's any way we could find him employment?"

"You know we can't fix things for every person we meet on the streets, right?"

"I do. But there's something about him that makes me trust he'd be worth the risk and investment."

Trace thought for a moment. "Okay. If we see Bruce today, I'll talk to him myself. If your gut feeling rings true with what I sense, I'll talk to Pastor. Our church custodian fell the other day and broke his hip. If Bruce is close to walking on his own, there's plenty for him to do around here."

"He mentioned only using the crutches to walk long distances, but I don't know when he'll completely heal." Camryn's heart sank. If they wanted someone who could do heavy physical labor around the building, Bruce might not be capable of fulfilling that role yet.

"We'll see what we can figure out."

"Thanks, Trace." Camryn glanced over to where Michael and Sherry sorted the latest donations of clothing items and fairy-godmother Martha—wearing a reindeer sweater—and her granddaughter filled plastic bags with toiletries.

Trace had mentioned that his pastor and a woman named Kate would also be joining them. The extra volunteers would make it easier to spend individual time with the people they served.

"It's nice that Martha's granddaughter is here today," Camryn said, applying mayo to bread slices. "I think teenagers care more about injustice and those in need than adults give them credit for."

"Kylie is a perfect example, and she's a natural with people on the street. She doesn't see grime, addiction, or dysfunction. Kylie views all as children of God." Trace stuffed a wrapped sandwich, an apple, and a cookie into a brown paper bag, then folded down the edges of the sack.

"I admire that in her because there have been times when I've struggled myself with what I've come across out there. If only we could all see people through God's eyes."

How did Trace view her? As a spoiled do-gooder? Camryn didn't think so—at least, she hoped he believed she was there with honorable intentions. "Martha and Kylie seem to have a good relationship. I've missed that. My grandmothers passed away when I was too young to remember them."

Trace glanced up at her last comment. "There's a lot of reasons they're close. Martha has raised Kylie since she was twelve years old. Martha's own daughter was a runaway, and Martha didn't even know she had a granddaughter until Kylie was placed in the foster care system and they'd tracked Martha down."

"How awful—and scary for Kylie to lose her mother and not know how or where she'd live. I can't imagine being that age and going through that trauma." Despite various conflicts over the years, her mother always had Camryn's back.

"By the time Martha was found and contacted, Kylie had been in the system for almost a month because she had no idea where her grandmother lived. She only remembered that her grandmother was still alive and living somewhere in Washington State. Kylie didn't even know her first name. She's sixteen now, and she's been with Martha for almost four years."

"Kylie's mother had kept all that secret?"

"Martha's open about her past life, so I know she wouldn't mind me explaining a few things. She and her husband weren't Christians while her husband was alive, and there were reasons why their daughter had gone on the run. It sounds like the husband wasn't a nice guy. Martha carried a lot of guilt for not protecting her daughter from his physical and emotional abuse. But having Kylie around has helped her heal—helped both of them heal."

"They have a wonderful story to share." To watch the pair now, Camryn would never have guessed they'd experienced suffering.

"They do." Trace smiled thoughtfully. "Everyone does, Camryn. But some don't realize it."

Camryn nodded. "When I first met Amy, she was different. Not at all like she was the night . . ." If only she could have the old Amy back—the friend who was funny and adventurous— the young woman who had many wonderful aspirations.

"Addiction can take over and make people do and say things. I'm sure she never wanted to hurt or disappoint you." Trace packed the last lunch bag. "I wish I could have done more that night on the street. You know, something that would have given her another chance."

"You did the best you could, and I'm grateful you were there." His presence had comforted her, even in the midst of chaos. "Would . . . would you like to join my family and me this Friday night? Around seven?"

Trace's eyes widened, and he took a slight step back. "What did you have in mind?"

"No pressure. It's just—we were planning a little get-together anyway, and since Amy has no relatives, we thought we'd also take a little time to remember her. Not a formal memorial service because it will only be us—my parents, my sister, and her fiancé. And since you were there—and then at the hospital—and took such an interest, I thought . . ." Maybe this was too much to ask, yet how could she not include him?

"Ahhh . . . I'm not volunteering with the Search and Rescue team this weekend." Trace gave her a small smile, as though warming up to the idea. "Yeah. I could come."

"Great. My dad's place is outside of Issaquah, so it's about a forty-five-minute drive from here. I hope it's not a bother to travel that far."

"Not at all. It will be nice to get out of the city for a while."

That was settled. Now to decide how much she should tell him about her family before he arrived.

Seven

W hat had he gotten himself into?

Trace parked his 2008 Honda Accord next to a BMW in an open area near the large home on the Tate estate. They wouldn't notice if he sat in the car for a few minutes and collected his thoughts, would they? It wasn't that impressive places were unfamiliar, but so far he'd avoided falling back into his former lifestyle—the very one his parents kept trying to convince him to return to in New York. The very one that led him to living on the streets like the people he was trying to serve now.

But Camryn had stepped out of her comfort zone several times that week to volunteer with his ministry, and she was doing an amazing job at acclimating. The least he could do was walk into that house and meet her family.

Trace beat his fingers on the steering wheel. Camryn had mentioned a few things about the Tates, but Trace had done a quick internet search before heading there. Her father, Jonathan Tate, was a respected plastic surgeon who currently focused on reconstructive surgery for accident victims. Camryn's mother, Eva, a former top model herself, owned her own modeling agency and worked out of an office in downtown Seattle. Liana Tate, her sister, was a special events planner, and her fiancé, Bryan Langley, was a gifted musician and songwriter.

It was while learning more about Camryn's family that

Trace realized her mother shared an unpleasant history with his dad.

Trace had considered backing out of the evening, but he didn't want to disappoint Camryn. Would she be upset if she knew? Maybe after all these years, the connection between their parents wouldn't be a big deal, but Trace wasn't willing to risk ruining the night for her. That information could wait.

The sun had already been down for several hours, but strategically placed lights offered a sense of the layout. Tall evergreens surrounded the estate. A small cottage sat to the left of the two-story home. Trace spotted a stable farther down the open property, behind the main house. Four evergreens—about six feet tall—were covered in white lights, and twinkling strands decked the bushes. The house and cottage were both outlined in glowing white. The setting looked like a Christmas card photo.

A peaceful spirit had settled there in the foothills of the Cascades. He could get used to the quiet. Most of the time he was able to block out the police sirens and other noises that came with inner-city living, but moments also existed when he craved sitting on a shore with no sound but lapping waves and sea gulls' cries.

The front door that held a hefty decorated lit wreath swung open, and Camryn stepped out onto the sizable front porch. She'd either heard him drive in, or she'd been watching for him. His reprieve was over. He'd agreed to this, and there was no backing out now. Trace stepped from the car, grabbed two boxes from the back seat, and made his way toward the house.

As a blast of chilly wind shot through the trees, Camryn hugged her upper body. "Hi. I'm glad you could make it. Did you have any trouble finding the place?"

Trace hiked up the porch steps. "No problem. The lit sign at the beginning of the driveway showed me the way. This place is so well hidden, it might have been hard to find it in the dark otherwise."

Camryn laughed. "Without that light, I'd have a difficult time finding where to turn off myself, and I lived here most of my life." She waved him through the open door. "Come on in. Everyone is anxious to meet you."

He held up his gifts—one smaller than the other. "Something to share with your family."

"Bakery Nouveau! The French bakery in Seattle—my favorite. How did you know?" She sounded delighted.

"I didn't, but the shop came highly recommended." Trace would thank Melissa again for her suggestion. "The larger box—pastries. The smaller one—macarons."

"Everyone is going to enjoy these. Thank you. It was very thoughtful." She gave him a warm smile, then shut the door behind him. "I'll take the treats, and you can get out of your coat. You can hang it in the closet over there," she said, nodding to his left.

"Greetings and Merry Christmas!" a male voice said in the background.

Trace closed the closet door and turned to face an older man wearing a masculine apron. His kind brown eyes and welcoming grin relaxed Trace.

"I'm Camryn's father." He extended his hand. "I'm glad you could join us."

Trace grabbed the man's hand with a firm grip like he'd been taught by his own father. "Thank you, Dr. Tate."

"No formalities, especially tonight. Please call me Jonathan." His focus landed on the boxes in Camryn's hands. "I see you come bearing gifts of the best kind." He peeked inside the smaller container. "Keep this up, Trace, and you'll always be welcome here."

"Dad, could you please take these to the kitchen? I'd like to introduce Trace to the rest of the family." Camryn smiled at Trace and shrugged. "He rarely has time to cook, but he loves it, so when there's a family gathering, he insists. We all pitch in."

Dr. Tate winked at his daughter. "Cleanup is all yours, honey." He smiled as though he and his daughter were sharing a secret. Or was there a joke on Trace? Maybe he'd been assigned kitchen duty along with Camryn. If so, he wouldn't mind.

"Follow me." Camryn led Trace down a short hall to a large living space with high ceilings and a massive stone fireplace holding a crackling fire. A tall, thin woman wearing a sleek red pants suit stood staring out the wall of windows that overlooked a backyard filled with white lights.

Decorative garlands were strewn across the fireplace mantel, and the pine scent that filled the air reminded Trace of hiking in the woods. Numerous candles lit up the room. Bing Crosby's soothing rendition of "I'll Be Home for Christmas" played through a sound system. A seven-foot Douglas fir sat in the corner of the room, near the fireplace and in front of one of the windows. Small white lights covered the evergreen, but it held no ornaments.

He'd expected an ornate, professionally decorated tree like the one his parents insisted on having in their home. *Home?* It never felt like one—more like a showpiece designed for a women's magazine. How many elaborate parties did his parents have planned for this holiday season? Whatever the number, Trace wouldn't be attending—his choice. Interesting... This grand room still felt cozy and welcoming. Was that due more to the design or the people within?

Did Trace find this overwhelming? Grateful her dad wasn't afraid to greet a stranger while wearing an apron, Camryn hoped Trace would discover that despite her family's success, they were normal. They still had challenges and dreams. They still hurt physically and emotionally. And they were still good people, despite what tabloids might print.

She liked Trace—a lot. He was different from the man she'd almost married. Camryn had been afraid to trust her own judgment after that failed relationship. But Trace seemed different. She couldn't imagine him lying to her or not representing himself truthfully.

Her fiancé had lacked honesty, but Trace seemed filled with integrity. She'd only met him a short time ago, but Camryn had witnessed his character and how he treated people, and it gave her hope that she might one day find someone she could truly love and who could love her. Trace had purpose in his life—something Camryn hungered for in her own journey.

"Come. Meet the rest of the family. They're expecting you." Camryn stepped farther into the room, and he followed, preparing himself with a deep breath. "Everyone, meet Trace Gardner."

The woman at the window turned, and as she came toward them, she set her glass of red wine on an end table. At the same time, the couple sitting together on the comfortable-looking brown sectional facing the fireplace stood. Camryn and Trace moved to join them.

Camryn put her arm around the waist of the woman in red. "Trace, this is my mother, Eva Tate."

"Nice to meet you, Trace." A knockout with short, styled silver hair, Camryn's mother must have been striking when she was her daughter's age. It was a no-brainer as to where Camryn got her looks.

He held her slender, cool hand in his briefly. "It's a pleasure, Mrs. Tate." Her ice-blue eyes studied him as though he were a specimen under a microscope. Did his last name make her suspicious? Did she notice any resemblance to his father?

"I'm Liana." The younger woman with long chestnut-colored hair had a genuine smile and golden-brown eyes that matched her father's. She glanced up at the man beside her. "And this is my fiancé, Bryan Langley."

"Glad you could make it." Bryan grinned and reached out with a hand covered with scars, and Trace didn't hesitate to grasp it.

"So am I." Camryn had been right to prepare Trace for Bryan's appearance. She'd explained that Bryan had tried to save several horses when a barn caught fire on his grandparents' ranch some years back. One side of his face had been severely burned, and even after numerous surgeries, he was still disfigured.

Bryan seemed so happy, his dark eyes almost twinkled. Was he always that jovial? Was his engagement to the pretty woman next to him the reason for his merriment? Was he a

Christmas fanatic? No. Trace sensed it was something within, something spiritual. Yep. That was it. Trace already felt a connection to the musician that couldn't be explained any other way.

"Dinner is under control," Dr. Tate said, stepping into the room without his apron. "I think now would be a good time to gather our thoughts and share some memories in honor of Amy. Would that be okay with everyone?" he asked in a more serious tone than when Trace had first arrived.

At the murmurs of approval, everyone joined together in a circle in front of the fireplace.

"I'd like to make a toast before we end. Does everyone have something to drink?" Dr. Tate held up a glass of wine as he glanced around the circle.

"Dad, I'll pour something for Trace and myself. It will barely take a sec," Camryn said as she broke the circle.

"Just water for me, please." There'd been a day when Trace would have sought out alcohol as soon as he stepped in the door to a gathering. No more. Those days were gone, and for good reason.

Trace wasn't a "normie." He wasn't like some people who could be satisfied and stop with one drink. One always led to another and then another. As an alcoholic, it no longer bothered him to be around people who drank. He felt it was their choice. They had a right to enjoy a glass of wine, but it wasn't something he'd ever be able to partake in. He'd accepted that he had a choice to remain sober or not, and he'd reached a point where he was content with abstinence.

A moment later, Camryn returned with two crystal glasses filled with water. She was unaware he was in recovery. Trace suspected she'd declined any alcohol to make him feel comfortable with his choice, and her thoughtfulness touched him.

Dr. Tate cleared his throat. "Amy Farell came into our lives when she was only sixteen, and in many ways became a part of this family. We tried to fill the empty holes in her life. In some ways we were successful—in other ways we failed. Regardless, she will always remain in our hearts."

The doctor's eyes shimmered from gathering moisture. "Bryan, you never met Amy, but I hope that as we share some memories, you'll get a sense of the young girl we grew to love. And Trace, we'll never forget what you did to try to save her and the interest you showed in her welfare after."

One by one, they told stories about Amy. Some were humorous, while others brought mourning. At times Trace felt like an intruder—a voyeur—of something sacred and personal. Yet other moments he felt honored and privileged to be a part of their memorial.

With the blazing fire lending its light to the room, Trace viewed each face in the glow—their tears, their smiles, and their laughter.

For what reason had God brought him to this place and this family? He genuinely liked them, but could he risk getting involved with these people—with Camryn—and being pulled back into the very environment that had almost destroyed him? He'd made a promise to himself to never return to that world, yet here he was, enjoying himself, and it terrified him.

Eight

"**D**inner was delicious, Dad." After years of observing her father's culinary skills, Camryn still remained impressed with how he could whip up a meal after a long day at the hospital. "I'll take care of the dishes later. I promise."

Liana grinned. "I'll pitch in too. It's the least we can do."

Their father could have shown off with a more complicated dish, but he'd chosen to serve a casual meal that included a choice of vegan or ground turkey chili, hearty rolls with butter, a lettuce salad loaded with other vegetables, and a peppermint ice cream dessert made with a chocolate cookie crust. Camryn gave herself permission to indulge. Peppermint was her favorite ice cream flavor, and well . . . it was Christmas. Her mother avoided desserts at all times, so she declined. Her loss.

"Thank you for dinner, Dr. Tate." Trace leaned back in his chair. "That's the best chili I've had in a long time, maybe ever."

"You're welcome. And remember—Jonathan is fine." His cell, which was placed on a buffet table nearby, rang with a soothing melodic ring. "Sorry. I need to get that. The hospital." He picked up his phone. "Dr. Tate here." His forehead furrowed, but he continued to listen as he left the room.

Camryn's mother dabbed her mouth with a red cloth napkin. "Always on call," she said with a hint of frustration.

They'd enjoyed a nice meal and conversation, and she'd

been on good behavior. Mom had worked on being more positive and supportive in the way she treated not only her family but everyone in general. Most of the time she succeeded, but there were still moments when she slipped into old patterns. Camryn chewed the inside of her bottom lip. Hopefully, with Trace there as a guest, her mother wouldn't start in now with negative comments about her husband or anyone else.

"There's an emergency at the hospital with one of my patients," her dad said as he rushed back into the dining room. "I'm afraid I have to bail on tree decorating."

"Oh, Dad, I'm sorry . . ." Liana said, sounding disappointed herself. "You've been looking forward to this all week."

"We can wait to trim the tree until another night." Camryn didn't want her father to miss out on one of his favorite traditions. They'd done the most important thing that evening by honoring Amy's life. Trace had met her family, and so far, everything had gone smoothly—another accomplishment. Camryn would sacrifice the tree if it meant her father could participate later.

"No, you all go ahead," her father said, wiping his brow as he gazed out the window. Clearly, his mind was already with his patient. "With busy schedules, it's tough to get everyone together. Leave a token ornament for me, and I'll find a place for it when I get home."

Liana gave their dad a hug. "We'll also leave the star for you to put on top."

"Thanks, Lee," he said, using her nickname. He reached out his hand to Trace for the second time that evening. "We appreciate you being here tonight. And I enjoyed hearing about what you're doing for the homeless. Not only with the Union Gospel Mission, which I've supported for a number of years, but also what you're trying to accomplish with building your own program. I'd like to learn more when we get another chance to talk."

"Thank you, Dr. Tate—Jonathan. I'd appreciate the opportunity to dig in deeper with you and share more details on what we hope to build in the next several years."

Camryn's mother appeared with her coat in hand. "I'll walk you out, Jon. I need to be on my way as well." She grasped Trace's hand. "It was nice to meet you, and again, thank you for what you did for Amy." Her eyes shone with moisture in a rare display of emotion.

Maybe her mother needed family more than Camryn or any of them realized. "Mom, are you sure you don't want to stay? It's been years since you trimmed the tree."

"You'll have more fun without me getting in the way," she said as Bryan helped her slip into her coat. "I'll enjoy my own tree while I finish a bit of work. Putting in an hour or two tonight will free up a couple of hours tomorrow."

"To do what?" Camryn was surprised at her disappointment at the early departure.

Her mother hiked an eyebrow and smiled. "That's for me to know."

First her dad, now her mom. Was the rest of the evening going to fall apart? Camryn's focus landed on Trace. He either sensed her looking at him or caught it out of the corner of his eye, because he turned toward her and raised both eyebrows. He seemed puzzled by what had just taken place—who wouldn't be?

Trace hadn't planned on staying into the evening, and he certainly hadn't expected to decorate the family tree, but after both parents split, he couldn't refuse when Camryn insisted. He removed the cover to a red plastic bin and glanced at the decorations inside. *Hmm . . .* No crystal or expensive designer ornaments. For the most part, they all looked homemade. This family was full of surprises.

Bryan walked into the room with a tray holding steaming mugs. Whipped cream topped all four. Liana carried a plate piled with the macarons Trace had provided.

"Hot chocolate, anyone? It's my special blend with a splash of cinnamon." Liana presented her treats to Camryn and Trace. "And these cookies are scrumptious."

Camryn laughed. "That dessert did me in earlier, so I'll have to wait. But you go ahead."

"With pleasure." Liana picked a green macaron and took a large bite, then she licked her lips. "I'll pay for this tomorrow with a long run, but tonight I'm going to enjoy them. Christmas only comes once a year."

Trace grabbed a mug, and after making his way past the whipped cream, he took a sip of Liana's creation. "This is pretty amazing."

"Right?" Liana grinned. "Thanks, Trace." She scanned the area. "We're missing something. Oh—I know. We can't forget to set up the nativity. I think it's packed in a green bin with a white cover."

"Remember when we lost baby Jesus?" Camryn reached into the red container and pulled out a clothespin reindeer.

Liana nodded. "Dad made a fun game out of searching for the figurine, and when we finally found Jesus buried under blankets in your doll bed, you explained that you wanted to keep him warm but had forgotten where you'd put him." She placed her hands on her hips and cocked her head. "So *we* weren't exactly at fault for the baby going missing."

"Oh, that's right." Camryn shrugged. "I was only three. Give a kid a break."

Trace felt a prick of envy. These two sisters seemed to have a close relationship and fun memories to share. As an only child, and with two parents who were absent most of the time, Trace had often felt alone—and lonely.

Liana finished her cookie. "Bryan, would you come with me to look for that bin in the storage room downstairs?"

"Sure thing." He hung a red glass ball on the tree. "But first—" He grabbed her, and they danced to "Rockin' Around the Christmas Tree" as he sang the lyrics along with the music piped into the room. At various points, Liana joined in with her own vocals, which weren't up to Bryan's talent, but she was having fun and didn't seem to care.

The song was nearly finished when the couple danced their way out of the room.

"Don't mind them. They're in *love*." Camryn held up a star made from popsicle sticks. "These ornaments probably seem a little silly, but my dad insists that we only use what we've made ourselves over the years. He says it's good to look back as we also look ahead to the future. That it's important to remember where we come from, and that no matter how far we roam, we'll always have a place to call home." Her voice hitched with emotion.

"I think it's a nice tradition." Trace could have benefited from a few himself while growing up. "What's their story? Bryan and Liana?" Was that too nosey? He was curious, but he also didn't want to pry into areas off limits. "Sorry. Maybe

I shouldn't have asked."

"It's okay." Camryn hung the simple star on a branch and smiled. "Bryan was one of my father's patients. He performed reconstructive surgeries on Bryan after the accident I told you about."

"The barn fire."

She nodded. "The building on his grandparents' ranch went up in flames. He happened to be there and was trying to get the horses out but got trapped inside. Bryan spent a long time in the hospital recovering, and when he was released, my dad offered him a job on our estate."

What would it be like to have the wise doctor as a mentor? Trace enjoyed being around Jonathan. Hopefully, he'd get another chance to spend time with him. "It was good of your dad to take a personal interest in Bryan."

"Dad was hunting for a caretaker, and Bryan was looking for work. After praying for God's direction, my father believed this was the place where Bryan could heal internally."

Camryn took an ornament with a small child's handprint from the bin and hung it on a bare branch. "Liana lived in the cottage on the property. She still does, and that's how she and Bryan met. They were both going through a lot at the time, but their friendship pulled them through, and over time, that relationship developed into more."

"You and Liana seem to be close too." Anyone who watched the two banter back and forth in fun couldn't miss the love they had for each other.

"We are now, but we went through some years where we couldn't be in the same room without irritating each other." Camryn gently rubbed a shiny gold glass ball she'd picked up. "That change came when I finally realized that my sister didn't have to be—nor did she want to be—an adversary. Bryan had a lot to do with that too."

"So it started with your dad listening to God and hiring Bryan. But in the end, that decision affected your entire family in a big way."

"Yeah, it did." Camryn sighed, then shrugged. "And sometimes it makes me wonder if anything I do makes a positive impact."

"Your modeling?"

"I still enjoy it, but . . ."

"You're looking for something more meaningful."

"Even if I am, what if God doesn't have anything else for me to do?"

Now she'd gone and done it. Opened her mouth and said more than what she'd intended. Trace was on staff at a church where he talked about his faith with people all the time. Would he think less of her if he knew her faith wasn't as strong as his? Not want Camryn to volunteer with his team?

"It's more like . . . I don't know if I believe that God sees me as being worthy or capable of doing something *important*." Even if Camryn volunteered a ton of hours and served hundreds of homeless people, would it be enough to prove that she was serious about her desire to make a difference somewhere?

After being hurt by the last man she was involved with, integrity had become critical to Camryn. But if she expected the truth from other people, shouldn't Camryn share her own as well, regardless of the fallout? Perhaps the time had come to take some risks and open up to Trace.

"Don't get me wrong. I've loved much of what has come with my career. I've been able to make a good living and travel all over the world. But I see how fulfilled my dad is with his job at the hospital. Every day he watches people start their lives over. He provides them with some hope. And not solely because of what he does for them physically. Whenever the door opens, and it feels appropriate, he shares his faith as well."

Camryn sighed. "I wish I could be more like them and my dad—assured of the direction God has chosen for me."

"Is that why you're getting involved with serving the homeless? You think you'll find your answer?"

"I don't know. Maybe. I was feeling restless before Amy found me. Right now I don't know if I'm feeling the urge to ease suffering because I'm being called by God or out of guilt for what I didn't do to save my friend. Probably both."

"When the time is right, God will let you know."

"I sure hope so." Camryn pulled a snowman made from Styrofoam balls from a box.

"Bryan and Liana have their careers, but they still make time to volunteer in the burn unit. The children there adore them. Bryan didn't mention it at dinner because he'll never brag about himself, but he's been working with an award-winning composer this past year."

She hung the snowman on the tree and stood back to see if it looked right in that spot. "They've written the scores for several films, and Bryan's role is to write new songs with lyrics. You've heard 'Love's Whisper' from the movie that was released a few months ago with the same title?"

"That's Bryan's?" he asked, sounding surprised. "It's being

played everywhere."

"It sure is, and we're hoping it will be nominated for some awards."

"I'm impressed."

"We're all proud of him." Camryn placed an ornament that contained an old photo on a branch, then studied the image for a moment.

Trace stood next to her. "Nice-looking family."

"Thanks. This picture was taken before we became broken." Not stated as a request for sympathy—simply a fact—a part of their story.

"Your mother doesn't live with your dad. But they're still married?"

"It probably sounds strange, but neither one could bring themselves to file papers. From what I can tell, they're working on their relationship, so who knows? Liana and I wouldn't be surprised if they got back together someday."

Trace pulled a tinkling bell from the assortment.

"My mom couldn't handle it when my dad's faith became important enough that he started focusing more on changing lives than making money. While she thought he was throwing away his career, he felt he was gaining far more. Neither could compromise, and in protest she moved out. She always preferred living in the heart of the city as opposed to spending time out here, so it suited her. But I've started to see changes in her too."

"Too?"

"Bryan's trust and faith in God has made a huge impact on my sister," Camryn said, lowering her voice to a whisper. "I've never seen Liana as content as she has been this past year."

"It's interesting to hear how people's lives are affected by choices they make."

"Good and bad. Both make a difference." Camryn eyed him. "What made you decide you wanted to work for a church?"

The other couple had returned with the elusive tub. "We found it." Liana raised her arms in triumph. "We can figure out where to put the nativity after the tree is finished."

Bryan set the container on the coffee table in front of the sectional, then added another log to the fire.

"We could use some help over here," Camryn teased.

"Coming." Liana joined them and poked through the bin.

"Hey, Trace," Liana said as she hung a painted ceramic angel on the tree, "you've gotten a good taste of our family, but what about yours?"

Trace had been rescued from Camryn's curiosity about his decision to work for a church, only to be put in a precarious predicament with Liana's question. He was doing everything he could to separate himself from his parents and what they stood for, and he wasn't ready to share that part of his life with anyone. "The short answer is that both parents live in New York, and I'm an only child."

"Are you spending Christmas with them?" Liana asked.

"No. We're not close." *Not even speaking at this point.*

"I'm sorry." Camryn sounded sincere. Of course she understood. It sounded like her family had gone through rough patches themselves.

"They worked a lot while I was growing up, building a business." Trace considered his response. "They wanted me to join them, so I gave it a shot, but it wasn't for me."

Trace would leave out the sordid details. It was part of his ugly past, and if he had any choice, that was where it would stay.

Nine

Along with other volunteers at the church that Thursday night, Camryn would participate in serving a hot meal to the homeless. She wanted to arrive earlier to assist with the meal prep, but prior commitments had taken priority.

Although it was only four thirty and dinner wouldn't be ready until five, people were already lining up at the side entrance to the building. Camryn drove past and headed to the back parking lot.

On Monday she'd flown to Los Angeles for a fitting with a designer, and she'd also completed a one-day shoot for a magazine, so she hadn't gone with the volunteers on lunch runs earlier in the week. She'd missed the team's camaraderie and the conversations shared with people they served. Instead of using *team*, they should come up with a name for the group. She'd give that some thought.

Camryn looked forward to catching up with Martha and Kylie, but she was especially anxious to find Trace. Since the family dinner at Dad's last Friday, intimate moments shared with Trace while decorating the tree kept coming to mind. It felt good to trust him with her hopes, her fears. He'd taken her seriously. But they'd also laughed and joked around. Trace made her feel *seen* and *heard*.

She slid out of her car and locked the door, making sure nothing worth ripping off was inside the vehicle. Not that hungry people would be on the lookout for something to steal, but it didn't make sense to tempt anyone either.

Good thing it wasn't raining, or everyone in line would be drenched before they got inside. Camryn's heart clenched. What would that be like—constantly fighting the elements, trying to stay cool on blistering-hot days and warm and dry on others?

The back door squeaked as she opened it, and welcoming aromas of food cooking enveloped her. Camryn made her way down a hall to the brightly lit kitchen where five people bustled around. She only recognized the gray-haired lady in a Santa Claus sweatshirt bending over an open oven door.

"Hi, Martha."

The older woman looked up with a grin, then closed the oven. "I'm glad you're here. Kylie will be thrilled to see you too." She turned and waved her arms in the air, getting everyone's attention. "Hey, folks. This is Camryn. She's another volunteer. When you get a chance, introduce yourselves."

Individuals acknowledged Camryn with a verbal greeting or a gesture, then they returned to their tasks.

Camryn inhaled, then grinned. "Something smells good."

"We have two ovens filled with chicken pieces, and they're almost done. Potato dishes are warming in the other two ovens. We're also serving corn, salad, rolls and butter, and a variety of cookies."

"Wow, someone has been busy. How many people usually show up for dinner?"

"It depends on where we are in the month and how their money is holding out. We'll probably have around a hundred tonight."

With no idea of where to dig in, Camryn was eager for an assignment. "What can I do?"

"Well, let's see." Martha put one hand on her hip. "You could join Kylie and Sharon in setting up the fellowship hall. Plates are already stacked out there for the buffet, and Kylie and Sharon are wrapping plastic silverware in paper napkins. Coffee is made, but would you pull cups from the storage area over there? We'll need paper for cold drinks and Styrofoam for hot."

"Sure thing." That sounded easy enough.

Martha checked her watch. "We only have fifteen minutes, so we'll start bringing food out to the tables lined up against the wall. People make a line, and we dish up their plate according to what they want. If you ask Kylie, she'll know what else needs to be done in the other room."

"I'm on it." Camryn glanced around the kitchen. "Where's Trace? I haven't seen him."

"Oh, he and one of the off-duty cops from church admit the guests. That's how we refer to them—as *guests*. We treat them with love and respect. But we also have to be careful. Trace and Jerod will greet them as they come through the door, and they'll check for contraband."

"Like what?"

"Alcohol, drugs, weapons of any kind. We need to keep a safe environment for the women and children—for everyone. And if anyone starts to cause a fuss while they're here, Jerod and Trace will escort them out."

Although Camryn thought of herself as quite experienced, having visited many parts of the world and been exposed to drug use, this felt different. More vulnerable for some reason. Maybe because children and women were at risk for harm. Maybe because in her world, drugs and alcohol were glamorized, and any possible danger was overlooked.

She carried several packages of cups to the large fellowship hall. Christmas decorations, way past their prime, lay scattered on tabletops in an effort to offer some holiday cheer, but they provided the opposite effect for Camryn. The centerpieces made from fake greenery, old bulbs, and other faded trinkets felt a little . . . depressing. But upbeat Christmas carols played through a small speaker in the corner of the room, and they created a cheerful atmosphere.

"Camryn!" Kylie waved as she rushed over to greet her. "I didn't know you were going to be here tonight."

"I'm glad to see you too." Kylie's enthusiasm always made Camryn feel welcome. "Everything in the kitchen seems to be in control, so your grandmother asked me to pitch in here."

"Awesome!" Kylie twirled her long necklace—a replica of miniature lit Christmas tree lights—around her finger. "They're bringing the food out now." She pointed to the large, covered silver containers placed on the long tables set up on the side of the room. "Those square containers over there are filled with hot coffee. We still need cranberry juice, the small cartons of milk for the kids, and pitchers of water. I'm on duty at the beverage station tonight. Would you like to hang out with me?"

"Sure. That would be fun." Camryn relaxed now that Kylie had made her first experience serving at the church more comfortable. Although tonight's mission was similar to the lunch runs, the setup was different.

Within a few minutes, the meal was in place, and the volunteers gathered in a circle to pray before the doors opened for their dinner guests. Trace literally ran in as they were deciding who would start the prayer. He joined hands with several people in the circle, nodded at Camryn, then bowed his head.

Trace had acknowledged her, but without a smile. Was he not glad to see her? He seemed to enjoy the time at her dad's last Friday night—at least, at first. The short memorial in Amy's honor was a little emotional, but Liana, Bryan, and Trace had hit it off, and they'd all had fun the rest of the evening. At least until the tree was decorated and they were saying goodbye. Then Trace had become quiet, thoughtful.

She hadn't talked to him since that evening. Camryn missed the Monday and Wednesday lunch runs but had texted and explained. Though thrilled to participate in his program, she still had bills to pay.

If she expected him to be understanding of her job requirements, he deserved the same. Camryn wouldn't take his cool greeting personally. Trace must have a number of things on his mind, given that the meal program was under his direction. As a friend, she could be a bit more sensitive to any stress he might feel in his role.

Camryn tried to focus on his prayer as Trace simply yet eloquently thanked God for everyone there. He asked a blessing on all coming for dinner that night, and he prayed they might be open to hearing how their spiritual needs might be met. Others chimed in with a few words, and then they broke the circle. Without a word to her, Trace left the room to supervise the door, and everyone else went to their positions.

Kylie and Camryn stood together, ready to pour drinks. People flowed into the fellowship hall. Some were quiet and subdued as they accepted their plates, while others chatted with the volunteers, and a few even made jokes. Martha seemed to know several guests by name.

A mother with three children—two girls and a toddler

boy—found a place to sit near the drink station. Then she asked the oldest daughter, about six years old, to get milk for herself and her siblings.

The girl walked shyly over to the beverages. She sucked on her lips, and her large, dark eyes revealed her apprehension as her gaze drifted between Kylie and Camryn. "Could I please have three milks? One for my brother, one for my sister, and one for me?" she asked as she held up three fingers and counted them off.

"You sure can." Kylie grinned at her. "What's your name?"

"Georgie. But when I get in trouble, my mom calls me Georgina."

Kylie laughed. "I bet you don't get into trouble very often, do you?"

"No, I try not to." Kylie's twinkling necklace caught Georgie's attention, and she pointed to it. "That's pretty."

"Oh, you like it?" Kylie held part of the strand up. "It makes me feel like I'm wearing a part of Christmas." She swung the necklace over her head and then draped it around Georgie's neck. "It's all yours."

The little girl's eyes lit up brighter than the bulbs on the string of jewelry. "I don't have any money to pay for it."

"It's a gift." Kylie took the girl's hand and led her to the side so other guests could continue getting their drinks. "Like baby Jesus was to us at Christmas. Only Jesus is much better than a necklace. Have you heard the story about his birth?"

"My mom told me he was born in a stable. That's kind of like a barn. And that was because his mom and dad didn't have anywhere to stay. Kind of like us. But that God took care of them, and she said he'll find us a place to stay too."

Overhearing the conversation, Camryn glanced over in

time to see the mother blink and wipe the corner of her eyes as she took in the exchange.

The cup of coffee Camryn poured for a quiet, older gentleman blurred before her. She attempted to smile through her tears so the man wouldn't think she was getting emotional over serving him plain coffee. "There's milk and sugar for the coffee right here, sir, if you care for any."

By his perplexed expression, he might have thought her odd, but then he caught sight of the interaction between Kylie and the young family, and he nodded. "This life is tough on the little ones." Then he poured a dab of milk and three packets of sugar into his coffee and shuffled off without another word.

Once the line of people had dwindled down to only a few stragglers, Kylie and Camryn took water and coffee to the diners remaining. Some people kept to themselves, and others had left as soon as they finished eating.

However, numerous guests lingered, enjoying a place to rest and chat. Camryn found some of the conversations fascinating. If she'd been anywhere else, she would have likened it to networking, as individuals shared resources where their tablemates could get assistance for medical needs, VA benefits, clothing, and shelter.

Camryn sat with a group of three women. Two sized her up and didn't say much. They probably weren't ready to trust her.

One woman named Lila appeared to be in her mid-thirties. Dressed in plain but clean clothes, a sense of pride emanated from this woman with dark curly hair and brown eyes. She must have believed Camryn was sincerely interested in hearing about her life, because she opened up and shared how she was close to finishing her degree—only one semester away—when her husband cleaned out their bank accounts and left the country.

"He asked me to put my education on hold until he finished college and established his career. We never had children, even though I wanted kids. Curt kept coming up with excuses for waiting to start a family or for me to go back to school. He became emotionally and verbally abusive. I couldn't take it anymore, so I finally stood up for myself."

"Good for you, Lila." How much should Camryn disclose? She didn't want to make the conversation about her. "I understand the courage it takes to speak your mind, especially when the guy is strong, and you're expected to cave in to what he wants. I've been in that position myself."

Lila's eyebrows shot up. "You have?"

Camryn nodded. "I wouldn't lie to you."

"You sure don't look like someone who has gone through anything like that. I'd expect men to fall all over you and give you whatever you wanted."

"See, that's the thing about verbal and emotional abuse—and sometimes even physical abuse—it's not always visible. If people want to hide it bad enough, it's possible for a while, but eventually the truth comes out in some form or another. But with time and help, it's also possible to heal." Camryn smiled and glanced at the other women. They'd remained silent, but they were definitely listening. "I'd like to hear more of your story, if you're willing."

Lila took a bite of sugar cookie, chewed it thoughtfully, then washed it down with coffee. "He finally agreed to me taking night classes at a junior college a few miles away if I paid the tuition myself. And if it didn't interfere with my job at the grocery store and taking care of the house."

One of the other ladies grunted. "And probably his *personal* needs too, I'd guess."

Lila didn't agree, but she didn't dispute the implication either.

"I never dreamed he'd leave, and I'd end up living in my car," Lila said, her voice thick with emotion. "I have a job, but my paycheck doesn't cover all my expenses. So I simply need a little help until I finish school. Being able to get a hot meal here at the church once or twice a week makes a big difference for me. I'm grateful—I truly am."

Hearing Lila's account humbled Camryn. No one should have to call their car "home."

Ten

"**I** hope to see you here again," Camryn said as she walked Lila to the door where dinner guests exited the church and returned to the streets.

"Next week. A person's gotta eat." Lila pulled a purple scarf from her bulging pack and draped it around her neck. "Thanks for listening," she said quietly. "Not many people care enough to . . ."

"Anytime, and I mean that." Camryn reached out, then instinctively pulled back. Lila might not welcome her touch. "Can I give you a hug?"

Lila jerked slightly, as if shocked by the request. "Ahhh, sure."

Camryn wrapped her arms around the woman and gave a gentle squeeze. Her slim body tensed, but she didn't pull away.

"Thanks. It's been a long time." Lila brushed her hand across her cheek, but not before Camryn spotted the drop of moisture sliding down her face. Lila hefted her belongings over her shoulder. "I better go and get some studying done at the library before it closes for the night."

"Sure. You take care." Camryn's heart went out to her new acquaintance. What would it be like to sleep in a car these cold evenings? Camryn would be more grateful when she climbed into her own comfy, warm bed that night.

Once Lila finished school, maybe Camryn could help her

prepare for job interviews. That idea sparked new energy in Camryn. She couldn't be pushy, but if Lila was open to it—a small makeover might give her the confidence crucial to landing a sweet position.

Camryn returned to the dining area and scanned the room. The remaining guests were mostly men, and she didn't feel comfortable visiting with them—at least not yet. Passing out lunches when she could approach one person at a time was different than joining a group of guys, regardless of their ages or how respectfully they might treat her.

Jerod, the security guard, remained at the church entrance the entire evening, but once dinner was well underway, Trace had left that position and roamed the fellowship hall. Camryn had caught a glimpse of him now and then as he made the rounds, appearing to chat with as many people as possible.

Kylie waved Camryn over to where she was sitting with a young woman with short raven hair. The girl in black could have been dressed for a role in a horror flick. Her eyeliner and shadow were darker than her walnut-colored eyes, and black lipstick accentuated her mouth. Where did anyone find that shade for lips anyway?

"Camryn, meet my friend Sam." Kylie sat to the right of the girl, and Camryn pulled up a chair next to her.

"Is Sam short for Samantha?" By the glare she received, Camryn sensed an edge to this teen.

"She doesn't like being called Samantha," Kylie said, saving Camryn from what might have spewed from Sam's mouth.

"Got it." Camryn smiled, but she didn't receive one in return. "You're on your own, Sam?"

"I do okay," she said, sounding defensive.

"I didn't mean anything by it. I'm purely interested in your story. We all have one, you know." Camryn didn't want to blow this. For some reason, she sensed it was important to Kylie that Sam liked her. "And I'm impressed that anyone can make it on the streets alone. It must take a lot of smarts and courage. I probably wouldn't last much more than a day or two."

Sam's gaze swept over Camryn, and she smirked. "Yeah—looking like that, you'd have no problem."

"Sam!" Kylie sounded mortified at the insinuation.

Camryn raised an eyebrow. "Thanks for the confidence." If this girl thought she was going to get under her skin, she'd be surprised. Without question Camryn could outlast Sam's insults, but she wouldn't return them. Camryn refused to continue the conversation through petty remarks. Those days were over.

Martha rushed toward them wearing a welcoming grin. "Hi, Sam."

Goth girl gave a halfhearted wave in greeting.

"Kylie, we could use extra hands in the kitchen."

The teen's shoulders slumped. "Gram, I wanted to spend more time with Sam."

It lasted only a few seconds, but Martha expressed a request to Camryn through her eyes. Camryn gave a slight nod to let the older woman know she'd received the message. Martha wanted her to have some time alone with Sam.

Martha kissed the top of her granddaughter's head. "Come on. I promise it will only take a minute, and Camryn is here to keep Sam company until you get back."

"Okay. I'll be right back, Sam. Don't leave without saying bye." Kylie got up and followed Martha to the kitchen.

"Those two are quite the pair, aren't they? I never got a

chance to know either of my grandmothers, so it's nice to see how much Martha and Kylie love each other." As Camryn relaxed in her chair, she spotted an unusual bracelet on Sam's wrist and pointed to it. "May I see your jewelry?"

Sam squinted. "Why?"

"Because I'm curious, and I've never seen anything like it before." Camryn held out her hand. "I promise to give it back."

"It's nothing. Just some old beads and weird stuff I found at the thrift store. I pick up cheap trinkets and make something out of them." Sam dropped the bracelet made from colorful and eclectic parts in Camryn's palm.

"This is a beautiful piece. If you're willing to create more, I'd be interested in purchasing some—matching earrings too. I'll pay you well, and I might even find more buyers for you."

"You're not kidding me?" Sam's tone rang with hope.

"Not at all. I'll be here on Tuesday and Thursday nights, so see what you can come up with. And if you need partial payment upfront for supplies, let me know. I trust you." Camryn had stepped out with faith, but there might not be any way to help without taking some risk. And perhaps reward would follow. For both of them.

"I'll give it some thought. Thanks."

"You're welcome." Camryn returned the jewelry. "Kylie sure seems to think a lot of you. Has she been a good friend?"

Sam shrugged, and her lips hinted at a smile. "She's all right, I guess." The teen slipped the bracelet back on her wrist. "She and her grandmother have offered to let me stay with them, but it's not for me."

"Why not?"

"Mrs. Strand is nice, but I'm not sure about all the God stuff." Sam fidgeted in her chair. "Kylie is kind of a goodie-

goodie. Naïve about things, you know. She even has a frilly pink bedroom."

"What about your own family? They must care about where you are, what you're doing."

"Not really. My mom's in prison for theft and drug possession, but she's getting out in five months. Maybe we'll live together again."

"What's her name?"

"Gloria—after the song about angels. Her parents called her Glory, which is stupid, because there's nothing glorious about her."

"And your dad?"

"Never met him."

"I'm sorry . . ."

"It is what it is." Sam crossed her arms over her chest. "I do fine on my own. I'm eighteen, so I'm too old for foster care, and I hated my last foster parents anyway. Escaped that house ten months ago."

"My mom never broke the law, that I'm aware of, but I know something about mothers who don't always show up in the ways we hope for. Although it may not feel like it, most of the time they're doing the best they can." Camryn somehow felt connected to the girl, despite having little in common. Maybe because like Camryn, Sam was searching for something more in life, even if she didn't realize it.

Trace shoved another tray of dirty dishes through the conveyor dishwasher, then filled an enormous sink with soapy water to wash the large pots and pans. It wouldn't be good leadership—and definitely not fair—to leave all the heavy cleaning to the volunteers.

Camryn marched into the kitchen carrying a sizable pan that held a few remaining pieces of chicken, and Kylie followed behind with an empty roll basket and a bowl with several wrapped butter squares.

They set their load on the counter, then Kylie explained cleanup procedures. Their chatter relayed a sisterly camaraderie—something he knew Kylie missed. Martha did a great job at providing a loving home, but she admitted to sometimes being out of touch with what young people her granddaughter's age enjoyed.

Trace had kept an eye on Camryn all night from a distance. From his vantage point, she'd been nothing but kind and patient with the guests, serving them at every opportunity with a smile.

She'd even spent considerable time with Sam, an older teen who'd been hard to reach but still kept showing up. Trace was curious as to what the two had talked about, but that was their business. However, that didn't stop the zing of hope that shot through him when he saw Camryn engaged in conversation with her. For some reason, he felt particularly protective of Sam.

He shouldn't have ignored Camryn earlier that evening. Sure, he had responsibilities and a ton of things on his mind concerning the meal program, but he could have spared a few minutes to welcome her, to express how much he appreciated her being there. Trace had missed her presence during the lunch runs that week, but he understood she had other commitments.

That was the real problem. He was getting used to her

being around as part of the team—*his* team. But how long would it last? How long before she tired of volunteering?

"Trace, did Camryn tell you the good news?" Martha bustled up next to him as he rinsed off a clean pot. Her grin almost reached both ears.

"Nope. Haven't talked to her all night." *Ouch.* It hurt to admit his negligence, and he winced at receiving Martha's glare.

"What's wrong with you?" She shook her head and pushed the palm of her hand toward him. "Never mind. I'm not supposed to judge." She picked up a dry cloth towel and wiped the clean pot on the rack with vigor. "I'm not going to say another word. It's Camryn's idea, so she should be the one to explain." Martha turned her back to the drying rack. "Camryn, tell our friend what you got in mind for a celebration."

Trace met Camryn's gaze, and his heart skipped a beat at seeing her cheeks flood with color. It wasn't overly warm in the kitchen, so the blush exposed emotion. She didn't seem the type to embarrass easily, but was she afraid to approach him with a suggestion? Trace wouldn't blame her after the impersonal way he'd treated her all night.

Camryn moistened her lips—those beautiful full lips.

"Tell him, Camryn!" Kylie's voice was filled with enthusiasm. "He'll be as excited as we are."

"Okay." Camryn took a deep breath. "I'd like us—the team—to throw a Christmas party here for the homeless community we serve."

Interesting—she'd said *we,* not *you.* "And when were you thinking about having this shindig?"

Camryn stood straight. "December nineteenth."

"It's already the tenth. That would give us only nine days." How could they possibly pull that off? There was enough to do for the holidays aside from putting together another event at this late date. "Maybe no one told you that we *wanted* to provide a full dinner on Christmas Day. But after a group of us listed our resources, we realized it wasn't feasible. We'd already accepted that decision a month ago. I don't see how we could possibly—"

"Trace, you aren't even giving it a chance." Kylie's disappointment rang in her voice.

Camryn put her arm around the teen's shoulder. "At least hear me out."

"Okay." Trace leaned against the sink, not missing that the rest of the volunteers stepped into the room to hear the public discussion. Maybe they should have waited to talk about the party in private. "I'm listening, and apparently, so is everyone else."

"Well, maybe they should. We are a *team*, after all," Camryn said with a gleam in her eye.

Trace nodded. "Yes, we are."

"So you originally wanted to provide a Christmas dinner with all the trimmings, and that's wonderful. But there's something magical about an evening party with candles—"

"We can't have a fire hazard on the premises."

Her eyes narrowed. "I have that covered. Battery operated. No real flame."

"Oh." By the daggers shooting from Martha's eyes, if he didn't want to be physically attacked by a mob, he'd better stop talking. "Okay, go ahead. Give me everything you got."

"I promise the party won't be a burden to you in any way. You only need to provide the space and spread the word." She gave him a warm, charming smile. "And part of that is to let everyone know that there will be an opportunity to share musical or other talents in a Christmas program."

Who could possibly arrange all of that in less than two weeks? His head ached from the stress that question put on his body. He leaned back farther and gripped the edge of the sink to keep from telling Camryn she was crazy.

"And the food? The cooking—the expense? Our budget won't cover another meal this month, and it's a little late in the season to raise more funds when many other charities are requesting additional support." He hated to be the voice of reason, and he didn't want to disappoint her, but sometimes dreams were pitted against reality. Maybe next year.

"Don't worry about that. Liana has connections with caterers, and my family has plenty of friends with money. If nothing else, I'll find a way to pay for the catering myself," she said almost defiantly.

There it was, one of the things that separated him and Camryn—*money*. She came from wealth and seemed to depend on it, while he'd turned his back on prosperity, wanting nothing to do with fortune. Money and the quest for more had almost destroyed his life, and now he was falling for someone who was very much accustomed to having it at her disposal.

This felt like trouble with a capital *T*.

Eleven

C amryn clutched the red paper cup in her hands. If it hadn't been full, she would have crushed it. After pushing Trace into holding a large Christmas party at the church, she'd barely slept an hour all night. And that reprieve came only after Liana had agreed to meet her first thing that morning.

Jazzed-up Christmas tunes and holiday aromas mingled in the busy coffee shop. The line for lattes, peppermint mochas, and various teas was almost out the door. Camryn and Liana were fortunate to grab a two-person table as soon as another pair vacated the seats.

"Lee, I can't do this on my own."

"Sorry, Sis, but you should have thought of that before you offered to provide a grandiose celebration. And in only two weeks."

Camryn sipped her spiced chai tea—feeding her emotions—the sweet drink in place of her usual black coffee. "I know. I should have thought it through." A big problem—her getting carried away and speaking before thinking last night. "And I guess I thought I could count on you to . . ."

"Bail you out."

"Planning events is what you do, and you're great at it." Camryn thought she could rely on her sister's guidance. Liana wouldn't refuse, would she? "It's such a good cause, I assumed you'd be happy to jump in."

"Even though, aside from spring wedding season, this is my busiest time of year."

"You're right." Camryn chewed her bottom lip. "I'm sorry. I shouldn't pressure you. I got myself into this predicament."

Liana picked up her gingerbread cookie, split it, and handed one half to Camryn. "Here. You're going to need the extra calories with all the work we have ahead of us."

"Really?" Camryn's spirits floated through the shop ceiling and out into the atmosphere. "You're not kidding?"

"On one condition."

"Anything." Camryn meant it. No matter what Liana requested, she'd agree to it.

"You do exactly as I say and don't question my instructions."

"Got it." Camryn smiled with gratitude. "I promise."

"I'll explore some ideas between now and Sunday. Come to my place for lunch after church, and we'll spend the afternoon working on details." Liana thought for a moment. "If possible, set up a meeting on Monday with Trace, his pastor, and anyone else they think should be included. We'll need their approval before moving ahead."

"I can do that." Camryn sighed in relief. Now that her sister was on board, everything would turn out perfectly.

"Camryn, I know your heart was in the right place. And I'm actually proud of you for wanting to do something nice for a group of people you don't even know."

"Thanks, Lee."

"But…" Liana picked up her cookie half and focused on the treat in hand.

"There's a *but*?"

Liana lifted her gaze to meet Camryn's. "Sometimes it can

be easy to jump into volunteering without thinking it through first. The opportunity may sound exciting or fun. *But* if it's not the right timing or we're not the right people for the job . . ." She raised her eyebrows. "It's not long before that role becomes a burden instead of a joy."

"Yeah. My restless night was a strong clue that I was in over my head."

"Don't try to be someone you're not, Camryn. Find where your own gifts can be used. That's when and where you'll find your passion, your energy—and your reward."

Twelve

T race and Pastor Brotherton had accepted Camryn and Liana's offer to coordinate a Christmas party for the homeless. They'd discussed some basics at a meeting, and the two women sounded confident in their vision. Since the men weren't interested in a long list of details, most of the decisions were left up to the sisters.

Almost two weeks later, despite several attempts earlier in the day to see how the final setup was coming along for the celebration that night, Trace had been interrupted by other developments needing his priority.

Now, any number of people could be assembling for the event about to start in the gym-size space attached to the church. Most days, it was used as a preschool, with classrooms separated by removable dividers, but on the weekends, Sunday school classes were held there.

Trace's knotted stomach had ached all day. He struggled with control when it came to his beloved outreach program. That issue could be blamed on his passion to serve, but maybe his feelings weren't as pure as he thought. Hopefully, the evening would be a success—for their guests and for Camryn.

Dressed in a new white shirt and a red tie, Trace opened a side door to the vast room. The unmistakable voice of Burl Ives singing "A Holly Jolly Christmas" flowed through the sound system. He surveyed the area filled with lights, music, and a crowd of people finding their way to open seats.

"You're here!" Kylie's smile was almost as bright as her new flashing lightbulb necklace, similar to the one she'd given away to a little girl. "Isn't this awesome?"

"Yeah, it's pretty amazing." How could they have done this much in two days? "You guys literally transformed this place into Christmas Land."

"The tree was delivered yesterday. It's so tall, we had to climb ladders to trim it." Kylie glowed as she pointed to the massive, decorated evergreen set up in the corner. "It's a secret, but Santa Claus is coming later to read a story to the little kids, and he's even bringing presents."

"Pretty cool." *Santa Claus? Presents?* He didn't remember any mention about jolly old St. Nick. Who did Camryn get to fill that role? And where were the gifts coming from?

Kylie waved to her grandmother, standing on the other side of the room, dressed in a fancy Christmas apron. "I better get back to work. It's almost time for dinner, and I'm one of the servers."

"Sure. I better check on some things myself." He'd thought it best to stay out of the way the last couple of days while Camryn and Liana took over the space. But seeing all the work gone into providing a beautiful setting, his absence nudged some guilt.

Trace had no idea of where or how he could contribute now, but he sure wasn't going to stand around like a wooden nutcracker and do nothing.

He greeted people as he made his way toward Camryn where she stood with Liana and Bryan. *Wow!* Camryn was stunning in that deep-blue dress. Her long blond hair cascaded over her shoulders.

"Hi," Trace said as he reached the trio. "Nice to see you,

Liana, Bryan. Thanks for all you've done."

"Our pleasure. Truly." Liana leaned into her future husband as he wrapped his arm around her shoulder and drew her close.

Bryan smiled down at his fiancé. "It's been fun." He leaned over and kissed the top of her head. "But my work isn't done. I need to check in with Michael on the setup for photos—"

"Photos?" Should Trace be impressed or worried that the party had grown into an extravaganza?

"I would have taken them myself, but since I'm overseeing tonight's entertainment, I asked a couple friends to take over that area. After dinner, my buddy Andy Sinclaire will take pictures of the kids with Santa, and Danny Woods will cover family photos over there at the holiday backdrop."

"See you later," Trace said, shaking Bryan's hand before he left to find his friend. Trace caught Camryn's eye. "Sounds like you have a full night planned. Is there going to be time to do everything?"

"I think so. Liana knows what she's doing."

"The schedule will be tight but manageable." Liana's focus moved to the crowd. "We'd rather keep people engaged in activities than have them get restless."

Liana checked her watch. "Five o'clock. Pastor Brotherton will give a short prayer before they start serving dinner. I'll let him and the caterers know we're ready."

"I should see if there's anything I can do to help," Camryn said as Liana headed toward the back where the catering company waited for the go-ahead.

Trace touched Camryn's arm to stop her from following her sister. "Please—wait a minute." There was more he wanted to say.

❧

Was Trace pleased with what they'd managed to put together in such a short time? Or was he irritated that she hadn't run everything by him? Camryn couldn't tell. In her defense, he and Pastor had given her and Liana permission to make some decisions on their own.

Trace squinted as if dumbfounded. "Who did you talk into playing Santa?"

"Pastor."

"TJ? He's willing to dress up in the red suit?"

Why did Trace sound shocked? "He was actually enthusiastic." Should she have asked Trace? "I'm sorry for not giving you a chance. I didn't think you'd be interested."

"No, that's not it. I'm surprised, that's all." Trace frowned, as though something unpleasant had come to mind.

"What's wrong?" Was he in some way disappointed? She'd been eager to share this evening with him, thinking he'd be happy and impressed by her efforts.

"I'm sorry. I shouldn't be acting like the Grinch. The decorations . . ." Trace sighed. "You've gone to so much work, but it all seems a bit extravagant. Like the expensive linens, centerpieces, the food—you're even using fancy dishes and goblets. Maybe all the money spent could have gone toward practical items that these people need. More food, toiletries, clothes—"

Camryn was forced to hold her response while Pastor Brotherton spoke a beautiful prayer of thankfulness and blessing over the crowd. Her eyes stung, and her heart ached at hearing Trace's accusations. Didn't he see there was another side?

The prayer ended, and Camryn pulled Trace through a nearby side door into an empty hall, where no one would overhear their conversation.

"Trace, I don't think any of this celebration is a waste," she said, trying to keep calm. If she released anger—born from hurt—she'd cry. "Why are you trying to limit their experiences to the lifestyle you think they're accustomed to? Or should ever have? Do you actually believe they're unworthy of nice things?"

Camryn's frustration simmered like a volcano beneath her cooler exterior, but she forced the feeling into submission. "I'm only trying to give them a Christmas to remember. And in terms of the cost, my father sets funds aside every year for ministries and charities. He would have been honored to cover all expenses. But he didn't have to because the caterer donated some supplies and services for the evening."

"I'm sorry," Trace said, adjusting his tie knot. "I spoke out of line."

"Apology accepted. But what about your hopes for tonight? Do you have any?" Camryn waited for his answer.

Trace pressed his hand against the wall and leaned into it. "I've been praying that all would go smoothly and the party would be everything you dreamed of."

An honorable answer. Why did it feel like an easy out? "I need to get back inside. I hope you can enjoy the rest of the night." Camryn opened the door, and Trace followed her back into the bedecked arena.

Martha rushed up to them, beaming. "Oh, this is wonderful, Camryn. Look at all the smiling faces. One lady was brought to tears, she was so overwhelmed by the beautiful decorations. And the kids—they can't stop asking about

Santa."

Camryn's spirits lifted. "You've all done your part to make this happen."

"Trace, you must be thrilled." Martha's enthusiasm practically exploded from her. "I'm sure Camryn told you about the ovens."

"The what?" He cocked his head and turned to Camryn. "I don't understand."

Of course he was bewildered. "I didn't get a chance to tell him yet, Martha." Camryn wasn't sure she wanted to at this point. "Along with the other donations, the caterer is allowing us to borrow some warming ovens. After we wrap up the party here, Pastor and I thought our street team could take several vans and deliver additional hot meals to the homeless camps. Liana will oversee the people who volunteered for cleanup, so we're free to leave whenever we're ready."

"I guess you have it all figured out." Trace rubbed his temples, as though trying to relieve some pain. "And the team is willing to do this after already working here all day?"

"They're all on board—Martha, Kylie, Sherrie, Michael— even Pastor Brotherton."

"And you didn't bother to mention this to me earlier? Last I knew, I was in charge of this outreach ministry. You taking over?" Now he sounded hurt—and angry.

"I'm sorry, Trace." He was right. In her excitement, she'd overstepped. "I didn't mean any disrespect. It all came together so fast. It wasn't like we had a secret meeting and planned to leave you out. You were busy with other things and weren't here at the time. That's all."

Trace nodded. "I know . . . I haven't been around to help." He rubbed his jaw, now covered with dark stubble. "I guess

I'm the one who needs to apologize—again—for letting my ego get in the way. Confession—pride is one of my flaws."

"Oh really?" Camryn raised her eyebrows in mock surprise, then she smiled. "Apparently that's something we have in common. I've been trying to prove myself, and in the process, I've made some blunders."

"It's not that I don't like the idea." Trace gave a sly smile and shifted his stance. "It's actually pretty amazing. Fill me in—*please.*"

"Dad thought there might be people who wouldn't feel comfortable coming into a church facility. So he arranged for additional meals ahead of time, without my knowledge. Earlier today the catering company offered to let us borrow the warming ovens, and Pastor accepted, quite enthusiastically."

Trace chuckled. "I bet he did."

One crisis averted. Trace seemed to have cooled down. Hopefully, as the night progressed, he'd relax and enjoy himself. But what other challenges would Camryn face before crawling into bed that night?

A turkey and ham dinner was served after guests were seated, and volunteers treated each person like royalty. Camryn managed to down only a few bites of salad, but she'd probably have more of an appetite once assured all had gone well.

Pastor Brotherton was a superb Santa, and Camryn was convinced he'd had as much fun handing out the age-appropriate gifts as the children had in receiving them. Family photos and Santa pictures would be available for parents by the end of the evening.

Kylie finished her last bite of chocolate silk pie and gave a sigh that whispered satisfaction. "That was *sooo* good. I could eat it every day."

"You're welcome to mine." It felt good to sit for a minute, but Camryn wouldn't linger.

"You don't like chocolate?"

"Oh, trust me—I do. I'm simply not hungry right now—too excited." That was an understatement. Adrenaline hadn't ceased flowing through her veins for even a minute. "Speaking of... I heard you're participating in tonight's show. I didn't know you played the piano until your grandmother mentioned it."

"I've been taking lessons for six years, but I'm a little nervous about performing in front of a crowd."

"You'll be wonderful." Camryn gave her young friend a side hug.

"Say a big prayer, because I'm going to need it." Kylie glanced at her cell and excused herself. "Bryan wanted everyone to meet about now to pray and get last-minute instructions."

A platform built across the end of the room would serve as the stage for the evening's entertainment. Liana had offered her expertise in arranging a lovely living-room setting that included a small Christmas tree with wrapped packages underneath—empty but still cheerful. A stuffed chair sat next to a fake but realistic-looking fireplace. Evergreens draped the mantelpiece. A small piano was also incorporated into the cozy set. Several microphones on stands stood to the side but within easy reach for anyone presenting an act or musical number—a mix of volunteers and guests for the evening.

Bryan slipped into the chair next to Camryn's. By the

worried expression on his face, something wasn't going well for her soon-to-be brother-in-law.

"Everything okay? If you're looking for Kylie, she left to find you."

"No, she's with the other performers. They're out in the hall, settling their nerves and waiting to pray before coming in. I have a section of chairs reserved for them up front."

At Liana's direction, a group of men arranged rows of seating for guests in front of the stage. What would Camryn do without her sister? She'd been instrumental in getting the night's details in place.

"I'm on the hunt for Sam." Bryan turned around in the chair and scanned the room. "She's in the lineup to sing 'O Holy Night' as the closing number. I was hoping you knew where to find her."

"I haven't seen Sam at all tonight." Camryn's stomach suddenly felt like hardened cement. "How could I have missed her absence?"

"You've had a few other things on your mind." Bryan drummed his fingers on his thighs. "Oh man, I sure hope the girl shows. I can fill in, but I'm telling you, Sam has a voice. And even though she was tentative about singing tonight, I detected some excitement too." Bryan jumped out of his chair. "I'm gonna make another quick search in here, then see if she's hanging outside. But we'll start on time with or without her."

Bryan had come far this past year, learning to be comfortable in public despite the scars covering one side of his face. He was still met by stares and rude comments at times, but he'd grown in confidence and didn't allow insensitive people to manipulate him or his feelings. Liana had a lot to do with that, and so did his blossoming career and strong faith.

Camryn desired the same for Sam—a new start that included a promising future.

But there was no way they could help the teen if they couldn't find her. Where was she?

Thirteen

"That's the last of it." Trace shoved the van door, and it closed with a thud. He never expected to pack warm food into the vehicle that night, and he was pumped to share the party's feast. "I think we're ready to hit the road."

They'd park in one location near downtown Seattle, close to where the homeless lived in tents, but still in an area where the police patrolled regularly and they felt safe in groups. The outreach ministry had built a solid reputation for providing aid without expectations or judgment, and the locals they often served would also be protective.

Trace climbed into the driver's seat of the first vehicle, Camryn sat in the front passenger seat, and Martha and Kylie sat behind them. Michael, Sherrie, and TJ would follow in the second van.

"A ton of food was designated for tonight's run. And those warming ovens . . ." The entire night had been pretty amazing already, and now this opportunity. Trace rode a natural high. "On a cold night like this, people are going to welcome a hot meal, Camryn."

"Hmmm?" She'd been staring out the window as they'd driven down the busy city street, but now she faced him. "I'm sorry. What did you say?"

"These hot meals will be appreciated."

"Yeah . . . I'm glad we can do this . . ."

Trace glanced in the rearview mirror at Martha and Kylie

in the back seat as he pulled up to a red stoplight. They were engaged in their own conversation. "What's going on, Camryn?"

"Nothing," she said wistfully, turning back to the bustling view of shoppers carrying bulging bags of potential presents, couples dressed for date night, and those with nowhere to go.

"You seem distracted." Her exuberance over their current mission had waned, so something else was on her mind. "Care to spill?"

Camryn shifted in the seat, appearing hesitant to pull her gaze from the activity outside the van. "I'm worried about Sam. Why didn't she show up tonight?"

"I don't know." Trace shrugged. "Sometimes people make promises because they don't want to disappoint anyone face-to-face. Even when they know that decision will still mean letting someone down." The traffic light turned green, and Trace stepped on the gas pedal.

"I can't believe that's true for Sam. Not this time." In the light from the city's glow, Camryn's eyes reflected deep concern for the missing young woman. "I'm afraid she may be in danger. I don't know how to explain it, except that I feel it." She pointed to her chest.

Here she'd put together an incredible evening—and from what Trace had observed, not for any recognition but because she genuinely cared about people. And instead of basking in the party's success, she was focusing on one girl's welfare.

Trace had admired her compassion toward her friend Amy when she'd collapsed from a drug overdose. He'd respected and appreciated Camryn's desire to jump in with the outreach program. But now, the way she ached for Sam, a troubled teen, Camryn had opened an inner door in his heart that had been bolted securely. Trace sucked in air at that revelation.

❧

Earlier, the team had parked the vans in one area and spread the word that hot food was available. Camryn was pleased that in two hours they'd passed out eighty-four free meals, and she looked forward to sharing that news with her dad. With dinners to spare, they stopped at the homeless camp built beneath an overpass nearby before heading back to the church.

Now in groups of two and three, they moved among the tents, the assortment of collected belongings, and trash that filled the air with a horrible stench. A few inhabitants rebuffed the offered meals, but most accepted them eagerly and with gratitude.

No Christmas lights were hung, no cheerful music played, no holiday cheer—what a contrast to what the team had experienced only hours earlier. A heavy sadness threatened to blanket the joy Camryn had embraced at the party.

"Bruce, I'm glad we found you." She grinned at the vet sitting in front of his faded orange tent. A small fire burned in a round, rusted bin about two feet across. Wisps of smoke rose from the short flames into the night—a fire that offered more visual warmth than physical heat.

"Now, isn't this a surprise!" Bruce slapped his knee, then stood to greet Camryn and Trace. "I sure didn't expect to see you here tonight."

"We missed you at the Christmas party, so I was hoping we'd get a chance to bring you dinner." Camryn handed him the covered disposable container that had warmed her hands from the damp, chilly air.

Bruce lifted the gift to his nose and inhaled, then he closed his eyes and smiled. "Turkey, mashed potatoes, and stuffing. The smell reminds me of my mom's kitchen. I will enjoy this. Thank you." He gestured to the space around the fire and tottered slightly. "Wish I could invite you both to sit, but I'm afraid I don't have any extra chairs. You're welcome to take mine, Camryn."

"Thanks, but I'm fine."

"Your ankle still giving you some trouble?" Trace asked, sounding concerned.

"You noticed I lost my balance for a second there." Bruce shrugged. "It's almost healed. I haven't done much walking. Haven't wanted to jeopardize hurting it more. But I'm off the crutches. Give it another week, and I'll be as good as new and can look for work again."

Camryn glanced at Trace. He didn't react to the vet's comment. Had he asked Pastor about the possibility of offering Bruce a job at the church?

"Please sit down and eat while the food is hot." Trace positioned the folding chair so Bruce could sit without bumping his leg against the bin holding the fire.

"Don't mind if I do." Bruce lifted the aluminum foil from the top of the packaged dinner, and Camryn unwrapped a fork and napkin for him.

Love in action—that described Trace. He didn't only talk about wanting to help people, he followed through. Aside from her father and Bryan, Camryn had never met another genuinely kind and selfless man like Trace.

"Bruce, have you seen a teenager around here dressed in black with short dark hair? Her name is Samantha, but she goes by Sam." Slim chance, but Camryn still had to ask in case

Sam had passed through there.

"Nope." Bruce dug his fork into the stuffing. "A group of teenagers hunker down on the other side of the camp, but I haven't seen anyone who fits your description. She a friend? A runaway?"

"Neither, but I'm worried about her."

The vet held his fork in the air and nodded. "You're a good person, Camryn."

"You got that right, Bruce. She is pretty special." Was that respect in Trace's tone?

"Thanks." Camryn held his warm gaze, which expressed more than admiration, but could she trust her perception? Was she also seeing affection? Dare she hope?

"You're not so bad yourself, Trace." Bruce chuckled, then his expression sobered. "So, why you two set on befriending losers like me?"

Trace knelt close to the makeshift pit and stirred the firewood with an iron rod lying next to it. "Is there anything wrong with wanting to lend a hand to someone who's going through a tough time?"

"No. Only curious." Bruce took another bite of his dinner and chewed slowly, thoughtfully. "Thought there'd be plenty of other things to do more fun than hanging out with the likes of us."

"It's simple." Trace smiled at the vet. "Matthew 25:40 tells us that whatever we do for others, in a sense, we're doing the same for Jesus. We're stepping in and being his hands and feet because he isn't here physically to do it himself. And that means no matter who they are, where they come from, or what they do. We love because he first loved us."

"I told Camryn when we first met that I'm not religious,

but my Evie always wanted me to have her faith." Bruce shifted in his chair. "I kept thinking there was plenty of time to decide whether or not I wanted to buy into that stuff about a loving God."

He held his fork as if to make a point. "Then things got even worse after she died, so I thought there was no reason to believe." Bruce scratched his stubbly chin. "Besides, what would God want with an old coot like me anyway?"

"It's never too late, Bruce." Camryn meant it. "I'm still learning what faith means."

"When you talk like that and show the kindness you do..." In the firelight, Bruce's eyes shimmered with moisture. "But what if I've been stubborn way too long? What if I've lost my chance?"

Now was the time for Camryn to risk being vulnerable, regardless of what Trace might think. It was more important to give Bruce hope than to impress a man she cared for. *Yeah. That's right. Admit, at least to yourself, that you have feelings for Trace.*

"I've made plenty of mistakes in my life, but my family and friends have forgiven me." Camryn dug her heel into the ground. No need to relay the ugly details. "I don't have all the answers, but God is being patient with me while I figure some things out. And I believe he wants to give you the same chance."

"I don't know . . ." Bruce sighed as though he carried a tremendous weight on his back.

"I do." Trace cleared his throat, but he remained silent for a moment, as though considering his words. "I've been where you are now, Bruce. I've been homeless, and I lived on the streets for over a year." He took a deep breath. "And I was in far worse shape, often drinking myself into a stupor."

Trace? Camryn didn't know what to say, so she stood there, numb.

"The point is, if I could start my life over, you can too." Trace stood, but he avoided giving Camryn even a glance. "Please think about it, Bruce. If you want out of here, I have a possible solution."

Fourteen

T race hadn't planned on bringing up his own homelessness in front of Camryn. That history wasn't a secret at Abundant Life, but his story also wasn't brought up in daily conversation. Since she attended a different church and only recently started volunteering with the outreach team here, it was unlikely anyone had mentioned his past. However, it felt important to share that personal struggle with Bruce in that moment, even if the information took Camryn by surprise.

Now, back at the church, would she be willing to stay a little while and talk? Or was she put off by his confession?

The team finished unpacking the vans. They'd store the warming ovens in the kitchen until they could be returned, and the other supplies would be shelved for future deliveries.

Camryn hugged Martha and Kylie as they said their goodbyes for the night. The two filed out the door, along with Michael and Sherrie.

TJ grasped Trace's shoulder, and he waved Camryn closer. "This has been quite a night. I'd like to say a blessing over you, if that's okay."

"Ah . . . sure," Camryn said, sounding hesitant.

Trace nodded. "Absolutely."

The pastor laid his other hand on Camryn's shoulder. "Dear Lord, we thank you for your amazing grace and love for us. We thank you for walking next to us as we work to serve you and those in need. I ask you to bless Camryn and Trace with the peaceful assurance that their efforts are never in vain. As they have poured into others, I pray that you provide them with all their needs, whether they be physical, emotional, or spiritual. In Jesus's name. Amen."

"Amen," Trace echoed.

Pastor Brotherton buttoned his coat. "It's been a long day, and I'm ready to head home."

"I can lock up, TJ. No problem." No problem at all. Trace was hoping for some time alone with Camryn, if she was willing.

"Sounds good to me. Thanks. I'll see you tomorrow in the office. And hopefully, I'll see you here on Christmas Eve, Camryn."

"I'm not sure where I'll attend, but thanks for the invitation. My family may want me to join them at their church. My sister's fiancé is singing for the service."

"I understand." TJ zipped up his jacket, said good night, and closed the door behind him.

Camryn took her car keys out of her coat pocket. "I—"

"Camryn, wait. Please don't go—not yet."

"It's past midnight, Trace, and we're both exhausted."

"I know, but I don't want to end the night without explaining."

"It's not necessary," she said, sounding weary.

"Please, Camryn. I promise this won't take long."

"All right." She offered a resigned smile and tucked her keys back into her pocket. "Where to?"

"The chapel." He led the way, and after opening the door to the small, quaint room with wooden pews, he flipped on a switch that backlit stained-glass windows.

"Oh, it's beautiful," she said. "Why haven't I known about

this place?"

"Maybe the right opportunity never came up." Trace moved to the center of the room, and Camryn followed him in sitting down on a pew. "I come here to think, sort things out—pray."

"I can see why." Her countenance relaxed, and she seemed to soak in the atmosphere.

"Thanks for giving me a chance to talk about what happened at the camp tonight."

"The part about you admitting that you were once homeless and you're an alcoholic?"

"Yeah, that part." *Stop stalling and tell her.* "I haven't been keeping it a secret. It's just not something I announce as soon as I meet someone."

"I understand."

From the tone of her voice, he believed she did. "I mentioned before that I joined my parents in running their business. And I told you that I knew the job wasn't right for me, but I agreed to give it a try."

"Yes, you shared that part of your life, but not much more."

Just spit it out. "I was also married at the time."

Camryn gasped softly but didn't speak.

"I had good reasons for not working beside my dad, but my wife took his side instead of mine. When I wanted to leave, they both pressured me into staying at the company. Job stress escalated my drinking, which was already a problem, but I couldn't hide it any longer. One thing led to another, and Nikki left me for another guy."

"That must have been painful," Camryn whispered, remaining still.

"The short story is that we divorced, and I chose to leave

New York and come here and escape. The more I drank, the more I didn't care what happened to me, and I ended up on the streets. At thirty years old, I'd already thrown my life away."

Tears shimmered in Camryn's eyes, but she didn't say a word.

What was Camryn thinking? Regardless, he couldn't stop now. "After a year of surviving day to day, I met a guy from the Union Gospel Mission. He saw something in me and didn't give up. Months later, I entered the twelve-month in-patient recovery program at UGM.

"Jesus became a friend instead of a myth, and through counseling and Bible study, I found my way back to a better life. And here I am—three years later—where I believe I can make a difference for other people who also need to believe they have value."

"I-I'm sorry you went through that, Trace." Camryn's eyes were filled with empathy, and her voice rang with sincerity. "I assumed you'd always had your life together."

"Not even close."

"Thank you for being honest," she said softly. "I haven't always been the best judge of character, and I've been be-trayed by so-called friends. When you challenged me on throwing a Christmas party, even though I promised to han-dle the details, I started to question your heart and motives for serving the homeless. I'm glad I was wrong."

"I misjudged you, too, Camryn, and I apologize." More confession. Hopefully, she'd understand. "I pushed back on the party at first because I didn't want you to think you could buy your way into feeling good about yourself. And now I'm embarrassed to admit it was more about protecting my own ego than exposing yours."

Camryn released a lighthearted laugh. "And we did talk earlier tonight about your inflated ego."

"Wait a minute. I didn't mention anything about it being *inflated*." Trace's shoulders relaxed at the banter, and he grinned. "But you're probably right again."

"Well . . . a healthy self-esteem at least, which isn't so bad." Her tone had grown serious again. "Trace, my last serious relationship ended in disaster because the guy misrepresented his character. His persona was a lie, so trust doesn't come easily for me anymore. But aside from my family members, you're the most truthful person I've ever met."

In this moment—in this intimate, holy room—Trace had never felt as close to another person. He'd loved his wife, but despite attempts to build a trusting relationship with Nikki, he often felt shut out.

Camryn's beautiful blue eyes held his, and he witnessed her belief in him. His heart pounded, and he wanted to draw her close and taste those full lips. But he wouldn't kiss her now—not when he hadn't told her the entire truth.

Trace opened his mouth, then changed his mind. She'd already taken in so much. What if she needed time to absorb what she'd heard tonight before she learned the rest?

Whether he was safeguarding Camryn or himself, he couldn't bring himself to disclose the last piece. He'd tell her about his family and why he avoided the rich and famous—but not tonight.

Fifteen

After what had gone into preparing for the Christmas party on Saturday night and then delivering additional meals later that evening, no one would have blamed Camryn if she'd slept in on Sunday morning.

But stirred inside by the love and generosity she'd witnessed throughout Saturday and then also hearing Trace share his personal story with Bruce at the homeless camp, Camryn had awoken early the next day, eager to join her father, Liana, and Bryan at their church service. Since she'd experienced evidence of God working in other people's lives, Camryn hoped he might have something wonderful and fulfilling in store for her as well.

The uplifting worship music had moved her, and one song about the Holy Spirit had created an unexplainable longing. The message encouraging people to believe they served important roles, regardless of their titles, felt as if the pastor had written it specifically for her.

Skilled in balancing humor with seriousness, he'd ignited laugher in the congregation when he asked what they'd do without a custodian to replace the toilet paper in the church bathrooms. What if no one took on the responsibility of emptying the trash cans, and the garbage continued to pile up for months? Simple jobs—no glory there—yet vital.

After the church service, Camryn spent the afternoon with

her father, talking about God. Something they hadn't done—at least not seriously—since her father's decision four years earlier to make his faith more important than attending occasional Sunday worship.

Not that her father hadn't tried to share his beliefs with her. In the past, Camryn had closed her heart and mind to whatever he had to say on the subject, but now she hungered to know and understand what he meant about having a *relationship* with Christ as opposed to believing he existed.

Monday morning, Camryn parked in the back lot of Abundant Life Church earlier than necessary, hoping to have a moment alone with Trace before joining the outreach team for that day's lunch delivery. Anxious to tell him what she'd grasped about God, and what her dad referred to as her *spiritual journey*, she got out and locked the car. Camryn still had questions, but she was learning.

The back door to the connected part of the church building where the offices were located was unlocked, as expected, and Camryn headed down the hall to find him.

She knocked on his half-open door. "Trace?"

"Come in." The man who swung open the door appeared familiar, but she couldn't place him. Tall, trim, and distinguished with graying hair at the temples, he wore an expensive dark suit. If Camryn guessed right, Gucci. "You're looking for my son?"

"You're Trace's father?" She didn't mean to sound doubtful, but he wasn't what she expected. This sophisticated man spoke firmly without a hint of warmth in his voice. Camryn couldn't mentally connect this person with the Trace she'd grown to care for—a lot.

"Erik Gardner, and yes, I'm very much his father, regardless of whether he admits it or not." Mr. Gardner eyed Camryn as though taking mere seconds to judge her. "The secretary said Trace went on an errand and I could wait for him here."

Where had she heard that name before—*Erik Gardner*? No, it couldn't be. That Gardner owned a chain of national and international luxury hotels. And he'd almost ruined her mother's reputation.

Now that she recognized him, Camryn wanted out of the room. "I'm sorry. I don't want to interrupt your visit with Trace."

"You work here at the church?"

"I'm a volunteer with one of the outreach teams that serves meals to the homeless. It's an important program run by Trace. You should be very proud of him."

"Proud?" Mr. Gardner sounded like the thought of Trace associating with the poor disgusted him. "Do you know my son very well, Miss…"

"Camryn Tate."

The older man raised an eyebrow. "Your mom is?"

"Eva Tate."

"I thought you might be her daughter. You look just like her."

"Yeah . . . you should remember my mother after what happened between you two."

"It's been sixteen years, Camryn. Best left in the past. The incident was a simple mistake."

"A simple mistake?" Did he believe that? "Mr. Gardner, those public photos hurt my entire family. They hurt *me*."

He shrugged, as though her pain didn't matter. "I'm sorry for whatever harm resulted, but your mother and I didn't do anything wrong."

"What *did* happen that night?" Her parents had never fully explained.

"Your parents were staying in one of my New York hotels. My wife and I had cocktails one evening with them after your mother pitched some marketing ideas using several of her models. A little out of the ordinary to bypass an advertising agency, but she was determined to get her business off the ground, and I liked that."

"My mother doesn't give up easily." Eva Tate had been described as ambitious, formidable, and pushy, but she always got the job done.

"I was restless that night and went down to the bar. Your mother was also having trouble sleeping. We sat, had a few drinks, and talked business until three in the morning. That was it," Mr. Gardner said, his gaze holding hers. "But we were alone, and at that late hour, someone took advantage of the situation and snapped photos. I'd made a few enemies through some business dealings at the time. Next thing we knew, a false story about an affair was published in several tabloids."

"I saw those trashy magazines displayed in the grocery store. So did kids from school." And they'd teased Camryn without mercy.

"Time passes. People forget and move on to the next scandal."

"*I* still remember."

Her mom and dad had fought about the rumors numerous times after the article's release. As an emotional twelve-year-old, Camryn's loyalty to both parents made her a wreck. She couldn't sleep, eat, or concentrate in school. Her relationship with Liana was fractured at the time, so she couldn't depend on her sister's support.

"Again, I'm sorry. But it appears Eva and Jonathan have moved on and done well for themselves. We can all learn from them, right?" Mr. Gardner walked over to the coffeepot on the counter. He poured a cup of coffee and offered it to Camryn.

"No, thanks."

He took a gulp of the steaming liquid. "Coming from a successful family like yours, you should understand more than anyone at this church what Trace has given up being here." Mr. Gardner's eyes narrowed. "Did you know that Trace has an MBA from Harvard?"

A master's in business, and he still ended up on the streets? "No, he's never said anything about his degree."

Trace had also never mentioned that the family business was more of an empire. She understood leaving a position that wasn't a good fit, but with his education, why not find another job? Had his divorce affected him more than he'd admitted? Where did his alcoholism fit into the story? And what about those tabloids that spread lies about their parents? Did he know anything about them?

What else had he neglected to tell her?

Sixteen

Trace, stunned to see his father standing in his office talking to Camryn, overheard the last part of their conversation. Imagining what she thought of him now, he avoided Camryn's eyes. "Dad, what are you doing here?" If only he'd waited to take care of that errand.

"I came to talk some sense into you, and I hoped you might listen this time."

Of course, his father had flown across the country because he still wanted Trace to fall in line with his objectives. It didn't matter what Trace desired—or needed.

"I should go and let the two of you talk." Camryn's eyes had lost their familiar sparkle. "Goodbye, Mr. Gardner."

Trace followed her out the door and down the hall. "Camryn, please wait."

"I'm heading home, Trace. I'm not feeling up to going out with the team today." Her fingertips brushed hair away from her forehead, then she tucked loose tresses behind her ear. "Please apologize for me."

"Camryn, can we talk for a minute?" She was clearly upset, so Trace didn't care that his dad was standing alone in the office. "*Please*. Tell me what's wrong."

She leaned against the wall. "Trace, I thought you understood how important honesty is to me." Disappointment filled her sigh.

"Our talk in the chapel on Saturday night . . ." Camryn's focus moved to the floor. "I was vulnerable. I felt close to you, and I thought you felt the same about me. It makes me sad that you didn't trust me enough to admit who you really are."

"Camryn, I'm sorry. I should have told you more about my family, but I've worked hard to live my own life." Trace propped his body next to hers. Maybe it would be easier to confess everything if he didn't look at her. "I almost told you in the chapel the other night, but I was afraid that after learning I was homeless myself for a while, finding out about the rest of my background might be too much truth to take in. But I planned on telling you. I promise."

"What *is* the rest, Trace?" she asked softly. "What else have you been hiding from me? Did you know about the tabloids sharing photos of your dad with my mom?"

"Yes, but I was fourteen and away at boarding school when it happened. At the time, other fabricated accounts concerning my father were being made public, so I was told the story about our parents wasn't true and I should forget it."

Trace's chest heaved as he grabbed a deep breath. "And I did, until you invited me to your family dinner. I realized the connection right before I drove out to your dad's place. I didn't say anything then because I didn't want to ruin the evening for your family." And truthfully, for himself.

"Trace." His dad stood outside the door of Trace's office. "I'm only here for a short time, Son."

"Go—spend time with your dad." Camryn pushed away from the wall. "I'm leaving."

"Can we talk later?" Trace was falling for Camryn. She was more than he deserved, but he wanted a chance with her. Hopefully, he could mend what had broken between them, but he couldn't do it here with his father staring at him.

"I don't know, Trace." She opened her mouth, then seemed to change her mind at saying what was at the forefront of her thoughts. "Bye."

Was she hinting that she was saying goodbye—and not only for today?

"Trace," his father said in a tone indicating impatience.

"Coming, Dad."

Trace hiked back to his office and shut the door behind him. He didn't need anyone overhearing their conversation. "That green chair is the most comfortable." Trace was tempted to sit behind his desk and keep a barrier between them, but instead he dropped onto the small brown couch.

His dad sat in the chair suggested and eyed him. "Your mother would love to have you home for Christmas."

"Hmmm . . . So that's your approach this time." Trace leaned forward and rested his arms on his thighs. "Mom will be busy with her parties. She won't miss me."

"That's not true. She wants to spend time with you."

"And that's the only reason you flew across the country? To invite me to Christmas dinner?" All the years he'd lived at home, he'd felt more of a nuisance than a blessing. At least until he'd grown older. Then he'd become an asset.

"I'm also here to talk some sense into you. Now that you're over Nikki and your rebellious season, it's time to get back to work at Gardner Enterprises. Stop wasting your efforts trying to save people who don't want to be rescued."

Always business first—the visit had nothing to do with wanting a better relationship with his son or having him home for the holidays. But Dad seemed more urgent than the last time they'd argued over Trace's decision. What would his father spring on him today? "I'm happy here, even if you can't see or understand it."

"What about your own family? I need you at the company."

"Dad, you've never needed anyone. And even if you did, I'm not the right person to follow in your footsteps. I don't want to wear those shoes. They don't fit."

"You'd actually choose *this* over a corner office in New York City and earning more money in a year than what you could spend?"

"Yes." Why couldn't his dad understand? Some people wanted to make a difference, to give back. Generous, caring individuals had helped Trace when he was on the streets, and in a small way, he wanted to honor them—he wanted to honor *God*.

"I'm not ungrateful for the opportunities I was given as your son," Trace said with as much patience as possible. "But you know I was miserable working at Gardner Enterprises. The stress, working too many hours, and the heavy drinking destroyed my marriage."

"And you believe you have a better job here?"

"I have real purpose. I see lives changed, and it's amazing to be a part of those transformations. My goal is to refurbish the building across the street. I want to create a shelter and educational facility for the homeless, where they can learn skills that will facilitate their transition back into society."

"What's stopping you?"

Trace's stomach churned. He could only answer honestly. "I haven't raised all the funds yet—but I will."

"I see." His father's piercing gaze challenged him. "What if you had a blank check?"

Trace's jaw dropped. "What's the catch?"

His father raised an eyebrow.

Why did Trace even ask? He'd watched his father play similar cards many times before during business dealings. "You'll give me what *I* want if I give you what *you* want."

"Trace, Marvin Anderson has cancer."

"What?" The news sent shock waves through Trace. He respected and admired Marvin more than any man he'd met in the company. Marvin was hard working and fair.

"He's resigning from his position, and I'd like you to take his place."

"Overseeing the international projects?" Once Trace's dream job—the one he'd aspired to move into when Marvin retired.

"Think about it, Son. With plans for a hotel in Sidney and Belize in the coming year, we need someone at the helm soon. You'd travel to both projects, and I promise you'd have full control."

"But what about my plans and what I want to accomplish here? I couldn't just walk away." Trace's mind was reeling.

"You could still be in charge of the renovation from a distance." His father made it sound like it would be no problem for Trace to maintain his involvement with the homeless ministry.

If he accepted his father's proposal, Trace would have unlimited funds at his disposal to remodel the building, and he could hire a project manager to oversee the job, as well as someone to run the programs he wanted to implement. And he could do it all without waiting or feeling the stress of raising money or burdening the congregation financially.

People's lives would be changed, but the reality of what his father was asking meant that Trace would no longer be personally involved. His responsibilities at Gardner Enterprises would make it impossible. And he would be expected to embrace the destructive dynamics, pressure, and unrealistic expectations he had successfully left behind.

"It's a generous offer, Dad, but acceptance comes at a high personal cost.

Seventeen

The wind blew a mix of rain and snow against Camryn's sliding glass doors to the balcony deck of her condo on Mercer Island. The small island on Lake Washington was connected to land. From here, she had quick access to Seattle by taking I-90 across the floating bridge, and on clear days, she had a view of the city from her home.

The clouds had prematurely darkened the sky that midafternoon and dimmed her Christmas spirit even further. It had already diminished after the disturbing encounter with Trace's father the day before.

Tomorrow night was Christmas Eve, and Camryn didn't want her sulking to affect the special evening with her family. She'd pick herself up by then—somehow.

Camryn lit the spice-scented candle next to the crystal tree displayed on the mantelpiece. An angel with soft, feathery wings smiled at her from the other end of the mantel. Camryn retreated to a soft blue chair next to the gas fireplace, where flames sent out a cheerful glow.

Her two-bedroom home was comfortable and offered plenty of space. At one time she might have been envious of the famous billionaires who also resided on the island, but lately, she'd been drawn to a simpler life.

An unexpected knock sounded, and Camryn set her cup of chai tea on the end table. She shuffled across the wood floors in her fluffy pink slippers, peeked through the peephole, and threw open the door.

"Liana, what are you doing here?" Camryn stepped aside, allowing enough room for her sister to enter.

"Well, nice to see you too." Liana made a silly face, then slipped off her coat. "Okay if I hang it on one of the chairs at the kitchen island? It's damp from the rain."

"Sure, that's fine. Tea?"

"Yes, please."

Camryn opened a cabinet door in the kitchen and grabbed a mug, then she filled it with hot water. "Chai or Jasmine?"

"Definitely chai. Sweet spices will hit the spot." Liana accepted the mug from Camryn, then followed her to their favorite spot in front of the fireplace, where she snuggled into her own comfy chair.

"I thought you were working today." Camryn sipped her own tea, now lukewarm. She'd reheat it later.

"I am. There's a big party about a mile from here tonight, and I've been there since this morning. The hosts didn't ask for much—just that it feel elegant but also relaxed and fun." Liana gave a quiet yet sarcastic laugh. Then she smiled and winked. "But they're nice, generous people, so I've done everything possible to fulfill their request."

"I'm sure it will be memorable, like all your events."

"Anyway, since everything is under control, I decided to take a short break and check in on you." Liana nodded toward the pile of overflowing shopping bags sitting next to the bedroom door. "By the looks of things, I should have come sooner."

"I know." Camryn's shoulders slumped. "I've been trying to break my habit of retail therapy, and I've done really well these past months. Obviously, I failed—again. But this time,

I'm donating everything to a women's shelter. That's why the bags are sitting there instead of stashed in my closet."

"What happened yesterday with Trace and his father got to you, didn't it?" Liana tapped the side of her mug. "You have feelings for Trace."

"I do . . . did . . . do . . ." Camryn set her drink on the table next to her, then hugged a decorative pillow to her chest. "But I feel betrayed, Lee. He challenged my motives for volunteering and throwing the Christmas party at the church, as though financial success kept a person from being sincere. Yet his family is one of the wealthiest in the country." She squeezed the pillow tighter. "It hurts that he wasn't up-front with me about a lot of things."

Liana tucked her legs beneath her and settled back into the chair. "You talked to Mom?"

"I called her this morning. She sensed something familiar about Trace but didn't make the connection to Erik Gardner. Who would believe his son was in ministry to the homeless?"

"How did she feel about you being friends with Trace?"

Camryn cocked her head. "Her reaction wasn't quite as negative as you'd think. Years have passed since that meeting with Trace's father, and aside from the painful fallout, she believes what she learned from the experience benefited her. It impacted how she conducted business going forward."

"Wow, that's a relief—that she didn't go ballistic on you." Liana grimaced. "That conversation could have gotten ugly."

"No kidding." Camryn wiped her brow with an exaggerated move. "Counting my blessings."

"So now what? Are you still doubting your reasons for getting involved at the church?"

"No. Maybe." At one time, Camryn could have answered

without reservation, but now? "I was feeling sure of myself, but then I see that pile of stuff over there. Was Trace partly right? Did I want to give a party so I could feel good about myself?"

"I think you're looking at this with blurred perception. There's no way Camryn Tate would give of her time or money freely without strings if she didn't truly feel compelled in her heart to do so." Liana's eyes shone in the way that revealed she was partially teasing but mostly serious.

Camryn couldn't fight the smile tugging at the corners of her mouth. "You're right—I'm kind of selfish that way."

"There's nothing wrong with providing tangible blessings. Sometimes, they can be as important as gifting someone your personal time." Liana sipped her tea. "The Bible says faith without works is dead, which means it's important to pray for people and be a listening, supportive presence in their lives. But if they need bread to survive, give them bread, not merely words."

"That makes sense."

"In your heart of hearts, do you believe Trace sees you as a shallow person?"

"No, but now our friendship has become more complicated." Camryn chewed on her bottom lip.

"Look. I understand why you're afraid to give Trace another chance." Empathy flowed from Liana. "The last guy you were involved with messed with us both—remember?"

Camryn nodded. She'd never forget.

"Bryan didn't reveal everything about himself when we first met either. It wasn't that he was being dishonest—he truly wasn't ready to share everything. I made the mistake of pushing too hard—and too fast."

Camryn hadn't forgotten how Liana had no clue about Bryan's history in the music industry until it was slowly revealed through a series of events.

"But when the time was right and he could trust my feelings, he opened up and didn't hold anything back," Liana said thoughtfully. "Maybe Trace wasn't ready to share his wounded past. And maybe he was afraid the truth about his family would turn you away."

The ring tone on Camryn's cell went off, and she grabbed it from the table next to her. "Hello, this is Camryn."

"Oh, praise God you answered! Camryn, it's Kylie." The teen sounded upset.

"Kylie, what's wrong?"

"Sam called from a burner phone. She needs help!"

"Where is she?" Camryn's imagination went to a dark place, and her stomach lurched. "Is Sam hurt?"

"No, she's fine, but a friend of hers has been sick for several days, and she's getting worse. They've been hiding out at the same homeless camp where Bruce lives." The words tumbled from Kylie, and her panic traveled through the phone. "Sam wants you there, but she didn't know how to reach you. I got your number from Trace, and he wants you to meet us at the church as soon as possible."

Camryn glanced at Liana, who stared at her with questioning eyes.

"Can you come?" Kylie's pitch rose, relaying her distress.

"Yes! I'm on my way." The memory of Amy on the cold ground and dying before her eyes flashed through Camryn's mind. They couldn't lose another person to the streets.

Eighteen

T race placed the first aid kit and a bag with other medical supplies in the van. He'd removed one bench seat to allow enough room for someone to stretch out in the back, but if necessary, he wouldn't hesitate to call 911 for Sam's friend.

He hadn't talked to Camryn for two days. She'd want to rescue Sam, but would Camryn drive to the church instead of going directly to the homeless camp? Trace had asked Kylie to reach Camryn, knowing she'd respond to her young friend before him. He couldn't blame her for being upset with him about not telling her that he was one of *the* Gardners. He'd wanted to call—many times—but felt it important to give her a little time to cool down before trying to explain further.

"She's here!" Kylie dropped several pillows next to the blankets in the back of the van.

Camryn stepped out of her blue BMW, dressed in a heavy raincoat and hauling a large canvas bag. "Let's hit the road."

All three climbed into the van—Kylie in the seat behind Camryn—water dripping from their outer gear.

Trace started the engine, and the wipers swished as rain pelted the windshield. "Thanks for coming," he said, facing Camryn. He was rewarded with a faint but genuine smile.

"I had to—for Sam," she said softly as she lowered the hood of her coat behind her head.

That was enough—for now. His personal desires weren't

as important as getting to the camp. Trace pulled out of the church parking lot, and they headed down the road, maneuvering the heavy Seattle traffic in sleet.

Tension filled the vehicle as they sat quietly, possibly lost in their own thoughts and worry. Trace should step up and lead. Wasn't that his role? "I'd like to pray before we get there."

"Yes!" Kylie said, sounding relieved. "Please."

Camryn nodded.

Trace gripped the wheel, turned on his blinker, and drove the van around a slow-moving car. "Lord, we don't know what we'll find when we arrive at the camp, but you do. Prepare our minds and hearts, and give us the knowledge and wisdom to make the right decisions. We ask that you keep us all safe from harm. We also ask that you protect Sam and her friend, and please cover them with your physical, emotional, and spiritual healing. In your name, Lord. Amen."

"Amen!" Kylie said firmly.

Camryn softly echoed the teen's response.

They parked close to the sea of small tents and makeshift shelters, got out, and grabbed the medical supplies. The sleet had stopped, but the damp air would chill a body to its core.

"Oh no." Kylie held a blanket close to her chest. "Sam was scared, and I was in a hurry to reach you. I don't know if their tent is brown or blue or green—"

"It's okay." Trace gave her a reassuring smile. "We'll find them."

The three searched the mass of sanctuaries, questioning the inhabitants only when necessary, not wanting to drag anyone out into the cold.

"Camryn. Trace. What are you doing here?" Bruce's arms

were filled with short branches and small wood chunks. He shifted his load. "For my fire, so I can heat up some beans later."

"Man, are we glad to see you." Trace gave him a light pat on the back. "We're looking for two teenage girls. They're living somewhere in the camp."

"One of the girls has short black hair and wears dark makeup." By the concern in Camryn's tone, no one could doubt that she cared about the teen. "The other girl is quite ill. Do you have any idea of where we can find them?"

"Same girl you asked about before?"

Camryn perked up. "Her name is Sam. Have you seen her?"

"No." Bruce nodded in the direction of his own residence. "But let me dump this wood at my place, and I'll take you to where the young people hang out."

"Thanks." Trace relieved him of his load, and in less than two minutes they'd dropped the pile inside Bruce's tent.

Trace, Camryn, and Kylie hiked behind Bruce with their heads tilted down while frigid wind smacked them in the face. They maneuvered around shelters until they reached the far edge of the camp not covered by the bridge.

A head popped out from a brown tent—Sam! Her eyes lit up at seeing them, and she stepped outside. "Thank God you found us."

Yes, thank you, God.

"My friend needs a doctor." Sam held the dwelling's flap open and waved them over.

"You guys go on. The place will be cramped as it is, and I'll only get in the way," Bruce said. "I'll stick around out here in case you need me."

"Thanks, Bruce." Trace nodded his appreciation, then followed Camryn and the girls inside.

Their sanctuary was small, and if it had been warmer, it might have felt cozy. The girls had set up two crates at the far end, where they displayed several Christmas decorations. The Santa Claus stood in a cheerful laughing pose, but the snowman's carrot nose was partially broken off. A shabby one-foot Christmas tree sat on another crate. Both wooden containers were turned on their sides and stuffed with books. A battery-operated lamp sat on a third box.

Trace knelt by the girl in the sleeping bag on the far right of the tent. "Sam, what's your friend's name?"

"Gina—Gina Mason."

Damp red hair clung to the sick girl's face, and her eyes were closed. Trace removed the thermometer from the supply kit and ran it across her hot forehead—102 degrees. Her pale skin indicated Gina's lungs weren't getting enough oxygen.

He carefully raised the top part of the sleeping bag from her thin body, lifted her arm from beneath the covering, and felt her pulse. Fever, shallow breathing, clammy skin. "Sam, how long has she been like this?"

"Maybe five days off and on. I came to invite her to the Christmas party, and she was sick then—mostly coughing. That's why I didn't show up at the church. I'm sorry I let you guys down, but I couldn't leave her alone."

Camryn touched Sam's arm in a comforting gesture. "It's understandable you wanted to stay with her."

"She was feeling better the next day, but last night she was coughing a lot and having the chills. I couldn't get her warm, and I got scared." By her tone, Sam was fighting to keep from breaking down in tears. "Today, it's freezing in here, but she's burning up. I couldn't let her lay there like that. I was afraid she was going to die."

Trace turned and sat back on his heels. "Sam, has Gina said anything about her family?"

"She's been in the system since she was five—now she's seventeen. Gina ran away from her last foster care family. She thought she was better off living on the streets, taking care of herself."

Gina stirred and opened her eyes. "What's going on? Who are you?" Terror rang in her voice, and she attempted to sit up. Trace, not wanting her to feel attacked, backed away.

Sam dropped to the ground next to Trace. "It's okay. They're friends. I asked them to come," she said as she gently guided Gina to lie down.

"No—I don't want anyone here. I'm fine." Gina barely got the words out before she started coughing uncontrollably.

Trace prayed silently until the coughing spell subsided. Gina was malnourished and seriously ill. There was no way he was going to leave without her. "Gina, you may have pneumonia, but we won't know for sure until you see a doctor. Regardless, you can't stay here. We can take you in our van to the emergency room at Northwest Medical Center."

"We'll gather all of your things, and Sam's too." Camryn glanced at Trace, and he nodded. "Gina, you'll likely be hospitalized, and we don't want you worrying about losing any of your possessions."

"What will happen to her after she gets better?" Sam twisted the hem of her coat with her hands.

Trace didn't miss the fear in Gina's weary eyes. "We'll figure something out, Gina. But right now the best place for you is in the hospital, where you can get medical attention."

"We need a plan." Camryn gestured toward the crates, stuffed bags, and assortment of other items the teens had collected. "It's too much to pack and haul everything out of here, including the tent, Trace."

"You're right. First things first. After we get Gina settled, I'll come back, and Bruce and I can load what's here into the van. I'll store everything at the church." Though the girl didn't own much, it wouldn't all fit in the vehicle now. However, what Gina did have was probably important to her, regardless of the value to anyone else.

"Wait a minute." Sam sounded exasperated. "What about me? I don't have anywhere else to go. I can stay and protect Gina's stuff."

Camryn faced the older teen. "I know you've taken care of yourself for some time, and you have street sense. And I know you're considered an adult, and I can't force you to do anything, but it would make me feel more at ease if you'd stay with me tonight."

"I'd take her up on it." Kylie grinned. "I bet her place is really nice."

Sam's eyes pooled. "For real?"

"I have a spare bedroom. It's yours until we can figure something else out."

"Yeah—sure. Thanks."

Trace wrapped Gina in a clean blanket and picked her up. He didn't want her wasting what little energy she had walking to the van. The rest grabbed what they could carry and headed back to the vehicle.

Hopefully, they'd rescued Gina soon enough. Not wanting to worry his companions even more, Trace hadn't relayed how sick he believed the girl was after spending days and nights without medical care. Although death from pneumonia was rare for teens, what else might the girl have contracted living under severe conditions?

And after losing Amy, what would Camryn do if Gina didn't make it?

Nineteen

Camryn turned on the sound system in her condo and chose an album of soothing Christmas carols from her playlist. "More marshmallows for your hot chocolate?" She held up the bag of minis.

"No thanks. I have plenty." Sam ran her tongue over her lips after taking another sip of her drink. "This is delicious. I'm surprised you have marshmallows. I thought you lived on carrot sticks and celery stalks."

Camryn burst out laughing at the image of herself gnawing on vegetables like a rabbit. "I *occasionally* indulge in treats."

Sam's grin vanished. "I'm worried about Gina."

Although it felt rewarding to see Sam more relaxed, even for a moment, concern for her friend was understandable. "Trace might have more information by the time he gets here."

"It was nice of him to insist on bringing dinner over."

"Yes, it was." Camryn had experienced a strangely familiar closeness to Trace while they worked as a team to get Gina medical attention. Still, dealing with a crisis was completely different from sharing a meal in her home. Camryn and Trace hadn't talked privately since his dad had shown up, so spending time with Trace *and* Sam tonight? Awkward.

But how could Camryn refuse after seeing Sam's eyes light up when he mentioned bringing food and possible updates about her friend? "He cares a great deal about people, and I think he realized that after the day we've all had, cooking might not be our top priority."

"Thanks again for letting me stay here tonight." Sam stared into the fire burning in the fireplace. "It feels..."

"Safe?"

"Yeah." Sam smiled. "And like Christmas. The candles smell like cinnamon. And your tree is pretty."

"Thank you." Camryn eyed her small evergreen decorated in white, silver, and shades of blue. She'd attempted a winter wonderland theme, and she'd nailed it.

Wrapped packages were piled beneath the tree, including one for Martha and another for Kylie. Tomorrow night was Christmas Eve, so she didn't have much time, but Camryn would find something special for Sam and Gina too.

She'd agonized about a gift for Trace, and her father had recommended the memoir *God's Smuggler*, by Brother Andrew. Initially keen to give Trace the book, she now felt conflicted. After their recent experiences—at the church with his father and then at the homeless camp—what was appropriate?

Someone knocked three times.

"Dinner must be here." Camryn peeked through the peephole, then opened the door to find Trace carrying several large bags with handles. "My goodness. Did you bring enough food for the building?"

Sam jumped up from her chair, and while she came close to dumping hot chocolate on the white carpet, she managed to not spill a drop. Camryn held her tongue. Flooring could be cleaned or replaced. Hurtful words—not as easily remedied.

"Did you hear anything about Gina?" Sam hugged herself. "Is she going to be okay?"

Camryn grabbed one of the bags from Trace, and he followed her to the kitchen where they set them on the island.

"A nurse from the hospital called as I parked. Talk about timing." Trace removed his coat, and Camryn hung it in the front closet. "She could only tell me that Gina will be fine, and she seems to like the social worker who is meeting with her at this very minute."

"When can I visit?" Sam frowned. "They will let me see her, won't they?"

"Tomorrow. During visiting hours."

Camryn's shoulders relaxed. "I can take you to see Gina. I'd love to check in on her too."

"Thanks, Camryn." Sam inhaled deeply, eyeing the bags. "I'm starving, and whatever you brought, Trace, smells delicious."

"Chicken fettuccine alfredo for the two of us, and garlic bread and a veggie salad for all three—black beans and pinto beans on the side for Camryn."

He'd remembered from the family dinner at Camryn's dad's that she didn't eat meat, and though a simple thing, it touched her. Maybe Liana was right about Camryn being too hard on Trace for not sharing details about his family. They were friends, not two people in a committed relationship, and it wasn't like she'd handed over her personal diary to him. As for what happened between their parents, could Camryn leave that in the past?

Trace opened one of the bags and removed covered containers. "I didn't forget dessert." He pulled a plastic container from another bag. "The middle school kids decorated cutout sugar cookies at the church to share after the Christmas Eve service tomorrow night, and Melissa packed extra cookies and frosting for us." He held up two bottles of colored sugar—one red, the other green. "And she threw in an assortment of decorations."

"That was kind of her." Camryn would find a way to thank the church secretary for her thoughtfulness.

"After Martha and Kylie explained all that happened today, Melissa hoped a fun activity might distract you from some worry."

Sam opened the plastic container and took out a cookie in the shape of a star. Her eyes glistened as she offered a small smile. "I've never decorated Christmas cookies."

"Never?" How could that be possible? Every child deserved to experience this tradition. Camryn couldn't fathom not participating in some kind of Christmas baking project while growing up. Even her career-oriented parents made it a priority during the holidays to spend time with her and Liana in the kitchen.

"My mom wasn't much of a cook, and she didn't like to bake. If we had any cookies, they were store bought. And the foster family I lived with said I was too old—I should let the little kids have that fun to themselves."

A pained expression crossed Trace's face, and his jaw clenched, but he didn't say a word. It obviously bothered him as well that Sam had been left out of the family's activity.

Camryn peeked inside the bag containing decorations and smiled at the treasure within. "Well then, Sam, this is the perfect opportunity for you to show us your artistic skills. But since we're all famished, dinner before dessert. Okay?"

"No way am I going to pass up fettucine." Sam studied a bottle of multicolored sprinkles. "Oh, these look fun." She set the bottle down. "Dinner first."

Trace removed the lid to a large salad. "I have another first for you, Sam, if you're open to it."

"Nothing can beat cookies, so it will have to be big."

"Hear me out." Trace leaned against a counter. "You didn't get a chance to perform at the Christmas party. Would you be willing to sing for our Christmas Eve service tomorrow night?"

Her eyes widened. "What?"

"I've already talked to the worship team and the choir director. They're both on board to back you up with instrumentals and vocals. You'd need to show up at the church for a sound check at one o'clock tomorrow, and they'd go through the song with you then. The choir was already going to lead the congregation in 'O Holy Night,' but they liked the idea of having you sing several verses solo."

"I don't know." Sam's eyes filled with terror. "It's such a huge responsibility. What if I'm awful? I don't want to ruin it for everyone."

"I would love to hear you." Camryn gave Sam a reassuring smile. "Bryan told me the night of the party that you have an amazing voice."

"Will you be there?"

Camryn nodded. "And I'll make sure you're at the church on time to rehearse. If Bryan wasn't singing himself tomorrow night at their church, I'm sure he and Liana would want to join us too." Camryn usually attended the Christmas Eve service with her family, but they'd understand. This breakthrough with Sam was too important to miss.

Twenty

T race would have been happy to sit back and watch Camryn and Sam create their cookie designs, but they insisted he participate.

He yearned to make things right with Camryn. She'd been polite all day, but that was probably because she was focused on the girls and didn't want to draw attention to any discord that he and Camryn were experiencing. She'd been a great partner in caring for the two teens but still distant when it came to him.

Sam finished off her third cookie and wiped the crumbs from her mouth. "Sooo good." She released a yawn. "I'm tired."

"It's been a long day, and everything is cleaned up." Camryn closed the door to the dishwasher. "Your bed is ready whenever you are, but you're welcome to take a bubble bath first, and you can soak in the tub as long as you'd like."

"Really? That would be awesome. Thanks." Sam grabbed another cookie from the pile. "Just one more."

"Good night, Sam," Trace said as she slid off her chair. This was exactly what the girl needed—a haven where she knew someone cared about her.

A dark shade of pink flooded Sam's face. "Thank you," she said quietly. "For saving Gina and for everything you've both done for me." Her lower lip quivered. "I-I don't know—"

"It's okay." Camryn wrapped her arms around Sam, and

the girl leaned into her, crying softly. "Sometimes emotions hit us out of nowhere."

Sam released the last of her tears, then she dried her eyes and left to take that hot bubble bath.

The time showed almost ten. Was it too late for Trace to stay a little longer? Would Camryn be willing to hear him out? Or would she be eager to push him out the door now that Sam was settled in another room?

Trace cleared his throat. "Camryn, I know it's a lot to ask, but I was hoping we could talk. My father the other day—there's more to explain." He hadn't wanted to sound shaky, so unsure of himself.

"I don't know . . ." Using both hands, she swept up her long hair into a ponytail, then she relinquished her hold, and the blond mane cascaded down her back. Camryn leaned against the counter and stared at the floor, seeming to contemplate his request for a moment. She lifted her head and released a weary sigh. "Yeah, sure. Would you like anything to drink? I was going to make some peppermint tea."

"No thanks." Maybe this wasn't such a good idea. She sounded exhausted.

"Sit and relax, enjoy the music, and I'll be right there."

Trace sat on the sofa across from the fireplace, praying for the right words, until she joined him.

She settled into the large matching blue chair and tucked her legs underneath her. "Okay, you start." Camryn avoided his gaze. Instead, she played with the string attached to the soaking teabag.

"I understand why you felt lied to when I didn't tell you about my family."

"Do you? *Really?*" Camryn sounded skeptical.

"Yes." He had to convince her he was being truthful. "You felt I judged you for having certain privileges. And because of that assumption, you might have believed that I saw you as leading an easy, carefree life. When in reality, I know you've worked hard to build your career. You're also one of the strongest women I've ever met."

Camryn moved her focus from her cup to him, and questions filled her eyes.

Showing vulnerability was uncomfortable for Trace, but he'd push through. "You haven't allowed your personal and professional life to interfere with caring for people who are struggling. You haven't felt any need to separate yourself from a world of opportunity in order to serve those living in one filled with despair. You've managed to find a balance—something I was unable to do myself."

"Trace, I'm still trying to find my way. And spending time with the outreach team—and you—has changed my life." She sat quiet for a moment. "What's the rest of the story? What made you leave Gardner Enterprises?"

"There's not much more to tell. Like my father explained, I graduated with my master's in business, and then I went to work for him. He approved of Nikki, so I married her. But I didn't love her like she deserved. The demanding responsibilities at the business created anxiety, my dad's expectations were unreasonable, and Nikki grew more unhappy."

"You said the other night she had an affair."

"It was my fault as much as hers. I was never home, and she felt neglected. My drinking got worse as job stress took a toll, and that didn't improve our home life either. We fought a lot—about everything. I'd pick fights with her to have an excuse to leave and find a bar."

"What happened after she left?" Camryn's question was barely audible.

"Against my wishes and recommendations, my dad decided to tear down low-income housing and build another luxury hotel in its place. Other locations would have worked as well, but he got a better deal on that particular property, and he found a way around legalities that would have slowed progress. Men, women, and children living in a hundred and eighty apartments were forced out of their homes in less than two months. He wouldn't even delay the project to give them more time to find other housing."

"Oh, Trace." She sounded as horrified as he'd felt watching it happen.

"After that, I was done with him and the company." Trace sighed. "I . . . ah couldn't do it anymore. I think partly out of guilt and partly to hurt him and myself, I packed up a few things, flew out here, and tried to disappear on the streets."

"I can't imagine what you went through."

"It was the worst time of my life, and I'm ashamed of what I did to survive." Nightmares no longer haunted him, but Trace would never forget what he'd learned. "God had something else for me though. Before I completely destroyed my life, I met a guy from the Union Gospel Mission. And you know the rest."

"You went through recovery, got sober, and were hired to run several programs at the church." Camryn tapped her cup with her finger. "Where does your family fit in now? Did your father convince you to return to New York?"

Trace shook his head. "He came with a new proposal. The head of the international division is resigning, and my father wants me to step in."

"Oh," Camryn said softly. "It sounds like a fantastic opportunity."

"It would open the door to numerous possibilities. I'd be in control of business operations all over the world, including overseeing the development of new projects. And in return, I'd have limitless funds to support any homeless shelters and programs I chose to create."

"What did you tell him?" she whispered.

"He wouldn't accept a decision until I took time to think about it. I'm supposed to give him an answer tomorrow." Trace hadn't expected to feel torn. "It should be easy, right? The things I could accomplish . . ."

"But . . ." Camryn raised her eyebrows.

"The thought of working in that business environment again almost makes me feel sick inside, knowing that I'd have to give up any personal involvement in the ministry. I'd feel like a teacher who created and graded tests but never got to enter the classroom, interact with his students, and teach."

"Then why not stay here?"

"I want to, Camryn, but is it selfish to decline my dad's offer? What if I never raise enough money to see my goals become a reality? What if I waste years watching that building across the street from the church crumble when it could have been used by people rebuilding their lives? And where does my pride come into this situation? What if God wants me to play a different role in the outreach program than what I envisioned?"

"I understand the struggle." Camryn twisted strands of hair around her finger. "But if God has given you a vision, especially one that isn't self-serving, doesn't it make sense that he'd provide a way to make it happen without making you miserable in the process?"

"That's my hope." Trace sat on the edge of the couch. "But what's most important to me right now, in this moment, is asking your forgiveness. I'm sorry I hurt you, Camryn. I apologize for making you feel that I didn't trust you enough to tell you about my family. I care about you, and I don't want to keep secrets." He held her gaze. "Can you forgive me?"

❧

Christmas sparked generosity in people's hearts, and her family had offered her grace numerous times over the years. Camryn had made plenty of mistakes herself. How could she not forgive Trace? They were friends, and he'd never meant to hurt or disappoint her. In many ways, despite the many benefits wealth had provided, they were both trying to find a path that would offer a more fulfilling life.

She set her cup down, reached over, and covered his hand with hers. "I forgive you, Trace." His skin felt warm to her touch, and surprisingly, Camryn didn't want to lose that innocent physical connection.

He offered a small smile, but his eyes conveyed something more. Desire? Yes . . . no . . . something purer. With reluctance, Camryn slid her hand away from his.

"I promise I'll do whatever it takes to earn your trust again." He stood slowly, clearing his throat. "It's late. I should go and let you get some rest."

Camryn walked with him to the door and withdrew his coat from the closet.

"Thanks for listening." Trace slipped into his outer gear. "I'm glad you're coming to our Christmas Eve service." He opened the door, then hesitated, as though trying to decide if he wanted to say something more. "Good night," he said quickly, and then he was gone.

Camryn turned off the living room lamps. The small lights on the Christmas tree, the lit candles, and the flames in the fireplace gave the room a soft glow. She dropped down onto the floor in front of the hearth and leaned back against the couch. Music still played quietly through her sound system. Despite the late hour and being physically drained, Camryn's mind whirled with activity. How was she ever going to sleep when the day's events played on repeat in her mind?

She'd forgiven Trace, but could she continue volunteering with the outreach team? Could she trust him again? Camryn cared deeply for him, but she'd been hurt many times before. She couldn't take another heartbreak. If he let her down again... Yet if anyone understood her need to prove something to herself, he did.

Sam must have gone to bed after her bubble bath. What was going to happen to the young woman? Despite Sam's ability to survive on the streets, Camryn wouldn't feel comfortable sending her back there. Sam's mom would be released from prison in less than five months, but then what? If they avoided counseling, didn't have jobs, or succumbed to pressures, they'd end up in trouble again.

Camryn believed in what Trace dreamed of accomplishing with the shelter and educational center. Though it wasn't the answer to Sam's current situation, it could offer hope to many people in the future.

An idea sprouted and bloomed like the first spring crocus poking up through the snow. It might take divine intervention for everything to fall into place, but wasn't an extraordinary event the reason for the season? Why shouldn't Camryn believe God might be willing to provide another Christmas miracle?

Twenty-One

That Christmas Eve morning, Camryn had risen early—a woman on a mission—determined to solve several problems. The notebook on her nightstand was filled with ideas scribbled throughout her restless night.

Phone calls, research, a visit with Gina, and shopping filled the day. Camryn had stepped out of Sam's rehearsal with the worship band and choir to answer an important call, but when they left the church, Sam felt confident about the song—even energized.

Because of timing, instead of driving out to her dad's estate and having dinner with her family, Camryn had picked up Italian food—Sam's favorite—from a local restaurant. Camryn felt dining at home with a calm atmosphere was best for Sam's nerves...and maybe for her own. She'd still celebrate their traditional Christmas morning and brunch with her family.

Now, time approached for the anticipated Christmas Eve service. Camryn shivered from the crisp night air as she and Sam made their way from the church parking lot to the main doors of the building.

The favorite deep-red dress she'd chosen from her closet was elegant but not overly dressy or flashy. Midi in length, the three-quarter sleeves, round neck, and full skirt all displayed scalloped edges. Previous years, Camryn had added several new holiday dresses to her wardrobe, but she'd declined invitations to parties this season. Stuffing her closet with more clothes wasn't necessary. Besides, Camryn felt pretty and sophisticated in this garment. Would Trace like it? Should she care?

Sam and Camryn stepped into the entryway, where people gathered in small groups, exchanging greetings and laughing. Garlands made from evergreen boughs hung over and around the door to the worship space straight ahead. Poinsettias, decorated trees, and carols playing in the background contributed to the festive feel that the buzz from people's chatter generated.

What would the evening bring?

So many questions demanded answers, but one regarding Sam and her living arrangements had been solved. She decided that sharing a pink bedroom with Kylie might not be horrible after all, and she'd accepted Martha's offer to live with her and Kylie, at least for now.

Camryn studied Sam. She took in all the activity and the gathering crowd. Sam wouldn't back out of singing a second time—not when people were counting on her, would she?

And hopefully, Camryn's expanding notion wouldn't deflate and disappoint people. Was it possible that out of her desire to fix things, she'd overstepped once again?

"Sam! Merry Christmas!" Kylie, beaming, approached them like a shooting star, with her grandmother following close behind. "Merry Christmas, Camryn. I'm glad you're here. Isn't it exciting? Sam's singing tonight. Wait until you hear her. She's *amazzzing*."

"Honey, I'm glad you're excited, but take a breath." Martha gave an approving nod toward Sam. "You look beautiful, Sam."

Kylie gave a quiet whistle. "You do clean up nicely."

"Thanks," Sam said, blushing. "Camryn took me shopping today. The dress is a Christmas gift."

Camryn, unsure of how Sam would take her offer, was pleased when it was accepted graciously. And when Sam had selected the knee-length dress with a modest boat collar, Camryn felt relieved she'd chosen appropriate attire for a church service. The full-length billowy sleeves were cuffed at the wrist. In place of black, the only color she wore, Sam had picked eggplant.

A long silver chain and locket accented the garment, and when Camryn discouraged Sam from wearing clunky boots, she'd settled on black flats. The biggest shock—Sam had foregone dark makeup for the evening. Her fresh, clean appearance was striking. But the best thing about the transformation—Sam admitted that she felt good about herself.

"You brought your stuff to stay over tonight, didn't you?" Kylie asked.

"I actually brought everything, hoping I could move in right away. It's all in Camryn's car." Sam glanced at Martha, as if to gauge her reaction. "Is that okay? I don't have much, so it won't take up a lot of space."

"That's wonderful, Sam." Martha smiled at her. "I'm glad you did. We'll be able to get you settled in, and the three of us will have a lovely Christmas morning."

Sam's shoulder's visually relaxed. "Sounds good to me."

"We should find a seat in the sanctuary before it fills up," Martha said.

"Sam and I have places saved up front." Kylie grinned. "I'm not much of a singer, but I was asked to join the holiday choir because they wanted more sopranos."

"Oh, Camryn, I'll need to slip out when there's a good opportunity." Martha looked at her apologetically. "I offered to help the hospitality team set out drinks and cookies for the reception following the service."

"That's fine, Martha." Camryn didn't miss the worry in Sam's eyes, so she mustered a large grin. "I don't mind sitting by myself, and it's only for a short time."

"All right." Martha shifted her oversized purse to her other arm. "Sam, I promise to pop in and hear you sing 'O Holy Night.' That's my favorite Christmas carol, and I'm not going to miss it."

While he greeted regulars and visitors and did his best to make all feel welcome, Trace had watched for Camryn, and now he spotted her across the room, heading into the sanctuary with Martha, Kylie, and *Sam*? Camryn had found a way to bring out the light hidden in that girl.

Tempted to catch up with them, Trace held back. As someone on staff at Abundant Life, he still had responsibilities to fulfill. Fifteen minutes later, the worship band started playing. People lingering outside the sanctuary filed in for the service, and Trace followed.

The lights dimmed, except for those required up front, but from the corner of his eye, he caught Martha sitting at the end of a pew. She motioned him over, appearing eager to talk to him. "Martha, you need something?" Trace asked quietly.

"I'd say it looks more like you're in need of a place to sit." She winked at him, barely speaking loud enough for him to hear above the music. "Please, take my spot."

"I can't take your seat."

Martha gave him a *don't turn me down* look. "I need to check on the coffee." She stood and stepped into the aisle. "You know . . . one of these days," she whispered, "we'll have to get one of those newfangled machines and make fancy drinks like they do in other churches." Then she took off before he could argue further.

Trace slipped into Martha's vacated space at the end of the pew next to Camryn. He leaned over near enough for her to hear him. "Merry Christmas."

"Merry Christmas, Trace." Those gorgeous eyes held his for only a moment, then she joined in singing, "Joy to the World."

The band kicked the tune into gear with a musician playing trumpet, which made the message even more joyful. When they'd finished singing several more carols, TJ welcomed members and guests to the service and said a short prayer. Then he asked everyone to greet those next to them.

Trace couldn't wait any longer. He touched Camryn's hand lightly to get her attention after she'd said hello to the lady next to her. "Could we talk after the service?" he whispered. "I have some news."

She nodded. "I have things to share with you too."

"Sam?"

"That's part of it." For the first time that evening, Camryn smiled at him. "As of tonight, she'll be staying with Martha and Kylie."

"They finally won her over." Trace chuckled quietly. "Proof we should never doubt the power of prayer."

People settled in to hear the message, so Trace and

Camryn sat down. The small space in their packed row forced their shoulders to meet. That didn't bother Trace—he embraced her nearness and her scent, although he had no clue as to the perfume she wore. What man would? Vanilla? Spice? He only knew that any time he smelled something similar, it reminded him of Camryn.

Hopefully, sitting this close didn't make her uncomfortable.

Twenty-Two

C amryn had never been shy about public displays of affection, but now Trace's shoulders innocently touching hers sent her heart into double time. The warmth of his body against hers felt . . . intimate . . . and different from anything she'd experienced before. She'd act cool. Not even the slightest hint of how he affected her would reach him.

Pastor Brotherton stepped from behind the stand, and using a head mic, talked about the night Jesus was brought into the world and what his birth meant for anyone who would believe in him as the Son of God. Camryn saw Mary as a real person, not purely a character in a Bible story, and she imagined the young teen having a baby in a stable—or a homeless camp—with only her husband by her side.

The pastor finished his message, and a small choir emerged from a side door, filing in to form a semicircle behind Sam. Camryn's palms moistened. Was this how mothers felt when their children played sports or performed in public? Did they all experience this nervous—but proud—anxiety? Camryn desperately wanted Sam to feel good about herself and confident about her talent.

The band played the intro, and Sam stepped closer to the mic. Camryn held her breath. But there was no need for worry. As soon as the teen opened her mouth and the first notes filled the large space, Camryn was mesmerized by Sam's tone and emotion.

O holy night, the stars are brightly shining,
It is the night of the dear Savior's birth;
Long lay the world in sin and error pining,
Till he appeared and the soul felt its worth.
A thrill of hope the weary world rejoices,
For yonder breaks a new and glorious morn!

Worth and the thrill of hope . . . Wasn't that what Camryn needed? Yearned for? To believe that she had more to offer than standing in front of a camera? Working with the outreach team had given her that and more.

Fall on your knees, Oh hear the angel voices!
O night divine! O night when Christ was born.
O night, O holy night, O night divine.

Camryn tried to discreetly brush her tears away. How she wanted to fall on her knees before God now. But here? In front of these people? She'd embarrass herself and Trace. Oh, to hear the angels sing. Perhaps she was in the presence of an angel's song. Sam's voice was filled with heaven's sweetness.

Led by the light of faith serenely beaming;
With glowing hearts by his cradle we stand:
So, led by light of a star sweetly gleaming,
Here come the wise men from Orient land,
The King of Kings lay thus in lowly manger,
In all our trials born to be our friend.

Was that part of his purpose? Did Jesus really want her as a friend? Camryn felt the tug on her heart. Yes, that was what she desired. No longer would she continue to push him away.

Trace closed his eyes and soaked in the music and words that flowed from Sam. There was no doubt in his mind that she was being used as a conduit by the Holy Spirit to flood the room with God's love.

He knows our need, to our weakness is no stranger!
Behold your King! Before him lowly bend!
Behold your King! Your King! Before him bend!

Yes, the Lord knew Trace's weaknesses—his stubborn pride for one. If he was going to serve to the best of his ability, some of his attitudes would have to change. Camryn was good for him. He cared for her deeply. She challenged him, and he needed her in his life—he *wanted* her in his life. Was that what the Lord also desired for him?

Trace stole a glance at Camryn. She stared straight ahead, but he didn't miss the tear trailing down her face. The song must be touching her heart as well. He reached for her hand, and she didn't pull away. Instead, she gazed at him, her eyes pooled with emotion. He smiled and squeezed her hand, reassuring her that he understood.

The choir joined Sam, and as the song swelled in volume, their blended harmonies wrapped Trace in what only could be described as wonder.

❧

The church emptied after attendees enjoyed cookies and hot chocolate. Sam went home with Martha and Kylie, and Camryn's heart warmed, picturing the three spending Christmas morning together.

Camryn waited for Trace to say his final goodbyes and lock the front doors. He'd asked if they could talk, and she had much on her mind as well. He led her into the small courtyard in the center of the complex, where a wrought iron bench sat next to an evergreen strewn with colored lights.

"I've never spent time out here." Camryn wrapped up in the blanket Trace had brought outside. "It's peaceful."

"TJ comes here every day to pray. At least, on days it's not pouring rain." Trace settled next to her. "It's kind of his place."

"It's nice."

Trace gently tucked an escaped edge of the blanket behind her shoulder. "Thanks for staying. I know it's late, but I wanted to spend a little time alone with you." He paused for a moment. "Last night you said you forgave me, but there's a difference in forgiving someone and being willing to have a relationship with him, even if it's a friendship. Is everything really okay between us?"

"Yes, we're fine." Camryn focused on the lit tree and took a breath. "A lot has happened in the last twenty-four hours, Trace. We may have some things to work out, but I don't want to lose your friendship."

"That's a relief!" He leaned against the back of the bench and pushed his hands from his forehead to the nape of his neck. "I couldn't sleep at all last night, thinking you might pull away because of my stupid mistakes."

"No, I'm not going anywhere," she said quietly and with more affection than she'd expressed before. "I've got a lot on my mind—things I need to explain." Camryn clutched the blanket tighter to her body. "But you go first."

Trace took a deep breath. "I'm not taking my dad's job offer. I'll find another way to fund the shelter."

"Good. Because I want to be a part of your vision, Trace. I want in—all in."

He jolted. "What are you saying?"

"I've talked to my dad, and together we want to create a foundation that will fund the shelter and educational wing." It was difficult to sit still and contain her enthusiasm as she relayed her ideas. "I'll continue modeling, for now, to help with finances. But I also want to get involved hands on. I'd like to teach classes for women on how to present themselves in a professional environment."

"I-I'm—"

Camryn laughed. "You can't possibly be at a loss for words, Trace Gardner."

"It shocks me too." Trace rested his arm on the back of the bench, and he slid a little closer to her. "You're an answer to prayer, Camryn Tate—more than one. My mind is exploding with possibilities, but I have a nice surprise for you too."

"You do?"

"It's all settled. Abundant Life wants to hire Bruce. As of January one, if he accepts the job, he'll be our new custodian. Housing will be available before then. I'm offering him the position tomorrow when I pick him up. Martha invited us both for Christmas dinner."

"Trace, that's wonderful. I'm sure he'll be pleased."

Not all gifts came wrapped in paper and bows. Sam had a place to live with Martha and Kylie, Bruce would have a job and an opportunity to get off the streets, Trace would have the necessary funds for the shelter, and Camryn had found a new direction for her life.

"Sam did an amazing job tonight," Trace said.

"That girl received so many accolades, she was glowing when she left the church." Camryn placed her hand over her heart. "I've never been that moved by a song." *Don't start crying again.* "I think I understand now what my family has tried to explain about faith and knowing God in an intimate way." She looked at Trace. "I want more of what I experienced tonight."

Trace took her hand in his and kissed it gently. "I'd like to join you on that journey. And I was hoping we could also see where our own relationship might go, if you're willing."

"I'm willing," Camryn whispered, then smiled.

Trace drew her close, then he leaned down, and his warm lips touched hers tenderly, removing the winter's chill.

Camryn wrapped her arms around his neck and embraced him, and his kiss went deeper.

Wet sensations tickled her neck. She slowly pulled away from him, and they looked up at the snowflakes gently bathing them.

Joyful laughter burst from within her. "Like the song. A night divine."

Trace grinned. "Merry Christmas, Camryn."

"Merry Christmas, Trace."

Dear Reader,

I hope you enjoyed this sequel to my contemporary romance, *By All Appearances*, which tells Liana and Bryan's love story. It was fun to revisit the Tate family and redeem Camryn.

The Christmas carol, "O, Holy Night," has always moved me. Just like what Camryn experiences, there's something about the melody and lyrics that tugs on my heart and makes me want to fall on my knees in humbleness and worship our King.

This song is also a message of hope—something that is so desperately needed in our world—no matter our financial status.

Seattle has a huge homeless population, and over the years, I've had opportunities through the Salvation Army and the Union Gospel Mission to serve on the streets and in the shelters. We've provided food, supplies, and special events, and I've glimpsed simple ways we can help and bless these people who struggle every day.

What might you do to help make someone's life easier? Brighter? It often doesn't take much.

Maybe—just maybe—we can change the world one person at a time.

"Truly I tell you, whatever you did for one of the least of these brothers and sisters of mine, you did for me."

~ Matthew 25:40 (NIV)

Acknowledgements

Readers…Your ongoing support often humbles me.

Annette M. Irby & Ocieanna Fleiss . . . My dear critique partners, I would not have become a published author without your friendship, encouragement, and honest feedback. I treasure the bond we've created over the many years of shared laughter, tears, and millions of messages exchanged.

Tina Boyd & Leann St. Germain . . . You continue to be my cheerleaders. I'm blessed to have you in my life.

My Family . . . Sonny, you have a servant's heart, and I'm looking forward to more adventures ahead, serving our Lord together. Brooke, Doug, Ana, Shawn, and Katrina—you all teach me much about sacrifice and giving to others.

God, my Father . . . Thank you for the privilege of sharing your love and grace through story.

Meet the Author

Dawn Kinzer, a mom and grandmother, lives with her husband in the beautiful Pacific Northwest. Favorite things include dark chocolate, cinnamon, popcorn, strong coffee, a good wine, the mountains, family time, and *Masterpiece Theatre.*

You can find out more about Dawn and her books by visiting www.dawnkinzer.com.

She loves to hear from her readers. You may contact her at dawn@dawnkinzer.com.

Other places to connect: Facebook, Goodreads, Pinterest, BookBub, Amazon Author Page, and Instagram

FREEBIE! Download "Maggie's Miracle"—a short story—as a gift when you visit www.dawnkinzer.com and sign up to receive Dawn's author newsletter sharing interesting tidbits about her books, photos, and other fun stuff about her writing world. Also available for purchase on Kindle.

By All Appearances

*An attractive special events planner
is determined to keep her distance.
A disfigured musician struggles to guard his heart.
By all appearances, both are destined to fail.*

Available in ebook and paperback on Amazon.
Available in paperback on Barnes & Noble.com
and Books-A- Million.com

The Daughters of Riverton

Historical Romance Series

Take a trip back to the early 1900s and spend time in the small farming community of Riverton, Wisconsin, where people find the courage to forgive, pursue their dreams—and love.

Book 1 – ***Sarah's Smile***

Book 2 – ***Hope's Design***

Book 3 – ***Rebecca's Song***

Though they follow a time sequence with some characters playing a role in every story, each book is a stand-alone romance featuring a different couple.

Questions that can be used for self-reflection or discussion are included at the end of each story.

Available in ebook and paperback on Amazon.
Available in paperback on Barnes & Noble.com
and Books-A- Million. com